PHARAOH
THE URBAN LEGEND

HARVEY C. LONG JR.

PHARAOH
THE URBAN LEGEND

CITIOFBOOKS, INC.
3736 Eubank NE Suite A1
Albuquerque, NM 87111-3579
www.citiofbooks.com
Hotline: 1 (877) 389-2759
Fax: 1 (505) 930-7244

Ordering Information:
Quantity sales. Special discounts are available on quantity purchases by corporations, associations, and others. For details, contact the publisher at the address above.

Printed in the United States of America.

ISBN-13:   Softcover   978-1-959682-26-4
            eBook   978-1-959682-27-1
            Hardcover   978-1-959682-28-8

Library of Congress Control Number: 2022920476

TABLE OF CONTENTS

CHAPTER 1

Pharaoh stood on the sidewalk of Village Green with one thing on his mind; nothing was going to stop him from getting money, absolutely nothing. His boney arms folded, his stare was fixed on the beat-up green Chevette leaving. It backfired and left a dark cloud of smoke in the middle of NE 15th Street. His best friend Boochie was leaving. Boochie had been moved to Tower Oaks with that girl Michelle. Pharaoh was still dealing with feelings about that.

He made his way around the laundromat and was soon halfway up the stairs when he heard his name, catching a whiff of that Gainesville green floating from somewhere around the corner. He kept walking, feeling a bit uneasy.

And so Monique followed him on up, strutting in her blue house slippers, her hazel eyes glued on him, her hair a little wild.

Pharaoh was shocked as he opened his door. It was just too late in the afternoon. As soon as she appeared he snatched her inside and immediately closed the door.

"Where da hell your baby-daddy at"?

"He ain't gonna be here for like the next thirty minutes," she said softly, rushing to wiggle out of her blue jeans, revealing her turquoise strappy lace panties. She took off her shirt and unfastened her black bra, breast plump and nipples luxurious as it fell beside her pretty little feet.

Then she stood there, a slight smile on her face, watching him, "We gotta hurry up!"

Aroused with a touch of unsurety, Pharaoh led her to his room, where she flopped down on his mattress and he reached on his raggedy dresser and grabbed a rubber. What was so special about him? Every since their first conversation it had been on and popping. But her baby-daddy was the baldheaded man that drove the red Malibu. He remembered the day he had saw them moving. It had only been a month ago. "Man…" he said, "What's up wit' you?"

"Nothing, I just need it real bad," she told him, taking off her panties, "Now come on. And how you been?"

"I been alright," he cried, then undressed. He was soon getting on top of her.

Now the sex lasted for ten minutes and Monique was gone. Pharaoh was in the shower thinking. She was cute. Five - four with thick thighs and a nice firm ass. Her lips were small and seem to give life to her cute little nose and doll–like face. But something was definitely up with her. And whatever it was definitely was far away from his mind right now. He was about to walk to the back and spend his last fifty dollars with Richie and Draco. He didn't have shit but a raggedy dresser and a mattress to sleep on, and a fan that decided it would spin around when it wanted too. He had a few pots and pans, and some silverware his momma had given him when she had pulled some strings to get him in his own apartment up front. And if she wasn't back there to her apartment, then she was somewhere in Crosstown smoking dope.

Soon, he was getting dressed – Dickie shorts a size too big. They even sagged when a belt held them up – white T and white soldier Reebok. He was on a mission.

Outside, a breeze was blowing along the balcony when Pharaoh left. He passed three girls and heard a grunt as he started trotting down the stairs. By the time he reached the bottom he had made eye contact with the two boys who were down there smoking. Then around the building was the baldheaded man just getting out of the red Malibu, *See, dis da shit I'm talkin' about.* He kept walking, reasoning with himself. *I need to leave her ass alone before I be in jail.*

Richie and Draco were about to smoke back there when Richie spotted Pharaoh coming. Kids were playing dodge-ball. Music was blasting from there open door. Richie was the fat one – big and light skinned, curly afro with curly chin hairs. He was sagging in fat boy shorts that were more than likely a fifty-eight in the waist. A huge t-shirt covered his sloppy upper half and green and white Nike covered his fat feet. He peered up the walkway at Pharaoh approaching, "There go dat skinny boy again, swearin' he makin' money cuz!"

Draco glanced to the left and continued rolling the blunt. He was a brown-skinned seventeen-year old with a pick in his mini afro. A flat nose bore his demeanor and he was two years younger than his cousin Richie, "Shit…" he said, "Pharaoh tryin' to get bread."

Knowing that Pharaoh was coming to buy dope, which was the only reason he came back there now, Richie went in his pill bottle saying, "What'cha lil' boney ass want?"

Pharaoh stopped in front of them and stared at Draco, "Why every time I come back here he wanna talk shit?" He looked at Richie. "I'm skinny and you fat. I'm lil' and you big. And you got the nerves to try to clown on me." He shook his head. "Now ain't dat some shit."

Richie grinned, "What'cha want?"

"I need uh jugg."

"Uh jugg," Richie cried, "I might bless ya lil' boney ass."

"Well, bless me fat boy."

Draco lit the blunt and looked at him, "Tryin' to get it, huh?"

"Gotta do something," Pharaoh told him, watching the pieces coming out of Richie's bottle.

"Nigga don't know how to sell dope cuz," Richie shook his head, "'Pose to have at least sixty wit' da shit I gave his lil' boney ass last night."

Putting the pieces in his bottle and walking off, Pharaoh told him, "Believe me, ya might see me again tonight fat boy."

"Yeah, and tell ya momma when ya see her to gimme my damn twenty dollars."

And so Pharaoh's night was restless. Cars were tricky and sometimes police rode through with their lights off. Or they would sit in a parking space between cars hoping to catch someone. Daylight caught him making another sale. Afternoon came by with another trip to Richie. And thinking about how Boochie had done him had him feeling a little down. He went in and came back out at nightfall. Then things started moving slow for him around 4am. However, he would walk back there and re-up with Richie before he called it in.

Weary and drifting down the sidewalk, Pharaoh was tired and in heavy thought, but when soft ticks crept up behind him he stopped and eyed the headlights of the slow moving car.

"You got dope," inquired the rusty voice of a man with stained teeth and one missing tooth. He had a bald spot in the middle of his head and little craters on both sides of his face. "What'cha looking for,"

"Sixty man, sixty."

Pharaoh hopped in the car – a little white Datsun. He caught a ride to the back, where he told the man to wait and soon bent the corner of Richie and Draco's building. He would wake Richie up. Knocking took a while. Finally, Richie opened the door with sleep in his eyes. Probably good their auntie Linda was in jail because she would've cursed him out this time of morning.

"You lucky it's your lil' boney ass," Richie told him, words dragging. It took him a while to come back, afterwards asking, "You seen ya momma lately?"

"Naw…"

Richie closed the door.

Back out to the white Datsun, Pharaoh handled his business and caught a ride back up. The man told him his name was Ted. And Pharaoh got out with the man swearing that he would holler at him. After he made his way towards the stairs he began slowly walking up. He was a little frustrated with no sleep.

"Pharaoh," Monique called. She had peeped out the window and had seen him.

He was in his apartment with the door wide open when she entered and closed it. Right there with his head tilted back on the wall, looking drained.

"What's wrong with you?"

"Nothin'"!

"Stop lying boy. Something is wrong with you."

Pharaoh sighed and looked around, "Shit… just tired of strugglin'."

Monique sensed his mood and walked closer, placing a hand on his chest, "It's gonna be alright."

He started frowning. Then he began looking at her like she was stupid. "What da hell you mean?" He walked off, "Look around, I ain't got shit."

Monique followed. It was obvious that he was going through something.

In his room, Pharaoh took his shirt off and slung it in the corner. He then began looking at her. "And you, I need to stop fuckin' with you." He pointed at her. "You got somebody."

"But I don't have feelings for him," she replied quickly with a puzzled look, "He my baby-daddy and we live together but, as far as love, it's not there," She paused. "Why do you think I'm fucking you? I haven't fucked him in two months."

"Yeah, yeah, yeah, but ya'll live together. And I'm supposed to be dumb enough to believe dat."

"Believe it or not but it's true." She folded her arms and started biting her lip. "It's just that we have a child together. I can't change that. I don't even have feelings for him." She walked closer. "But I have some feelings for you."

"And what'cha gon' do when he catch'cha?" Frowning, his forehead wrinkled and he shot her that straight look. "Ya ass left da other day and about ten minutes later he was here. He come to me wit' dat bullshit," Pharaoh pointed at himself, "I ain't even much having it."

"Just let me handle it, okay. I know what I'm doing."

I bet you do. Have uh nigga in jail wit' uh murder charge. "You need to go." He pushed her back.

"What's wrong with you?"

"Money on my mind, not pussy,"

Shocked, Monique swallowed the pain of his statement. "You didn't even have to say it like that but I understand." She walked off. It had hurt her. Slowly, tears began to form.

CHAPTER 2

Teary eyed, Monique closed the door of Pharaoh's apartment and soon trotted down the steps to hers. After locking the door and checking on her daughter, Sakena, she got in bed crying. A lot was on her mind. The long sense of getting away bothered her, but she couldn't. Where would she go? Back to Ft. Myers with her alcoholic father who use to abuse her. She hadn't been back there in almost four and a half years. She had been staying with Melvin, the one who'd brought her away from the mess, and it turned out now that he was doing the same thing. She had feelings for him but they weren't deep anymore. The spark had left several months ago, descending into a mere trace of history. Was it her fault that he was putting his hands on her every time he did get frustrated and angry? She was tired of her daughter seeing them fight and tired of being abused. Even at his mother's house she had been longing to get away. But he'd saved some money and had bought some cheap furniture and had moved them out there. His mother had grown tired – all the arguing and fighting and living like married people under her roof. And she couldn't blame Tina after all that time.

Soaking her tears up with her pillow, she tried to get Pharaoh off of her mind, but she couldn't. It wasn't the sex that made him great. It was his character. The way he appeared – skinny, boney. It turned her on. The way he talked. The funny things he said. She loved everything about him. Yet, what he'd told her had hurt her deeply. She couldn't help that it seemed that way. Bottom line was that she had sexual needs that needed nurturing and, every time she did get the chance, she took advantage of it by doing herself a favor. She knew it really wasn't the way he thought it was.

Stuck in the pain of remembering Pharaoh's words, Monique pulled the covers over her head and cried, until she finally got a grip on her emotions; remembering the beauty of their first conversation. Yes, their first conversation! The evening she first stepped out to stop these two little boys from fighting in front of her door. The evening she was bombed rushed by a boy because she was new out there; although she didn't know who he thought she was. It was the same evening that she had first laid eyes on him. He had been walking up the stairs. The moment she knew she liked him because he seemed lost in his own world.

Monique smiled and rolled over in the covers, remembering their first conversation word for word. She had spoken first.

"Hey, how you doing,"

"Bad as uh motherfucka"!

"And why is that?" She relived the memory of how he'd stopped and had stared down at her.

"'Cause I'm po', if I had money then I'll be doing damn good," Laughing to herself at the funny way he had said that, Monique pulled the covers of her head, thinking it was darker that way and she could see him clearer, "And what's your name?" she recalled asking him, clearly seeing it like yesterday.

"Pharaoh"!

"And why they call you that?" Then the memory of how he came back down the stairs, how he folded his arms with a steady look at her, dressed in a t-shirt, creased Dickie jeans, and white Nike – looking at her with those handsome eyes, his handsome appearance, making her feel like a little girl, unaware that she had been about to laugh.

"'Cause when I was small I use to run 'round in my spiderman and flintstone drawers hollarin' about I'm Pharaoh of Egypt. I use to love the movies about Egypt so my momma started callin' me Pharaoh. Dat's how I got this name, in spiderman and flintstone drawers. Remember that, I'm Pharaoh."

Monique laughed to herself until she thought of his condition. When she had first snuck up there to his apartment, she had been blowed. He was right. He barely had anything. But she didn't mind and, he hadn't been embarrassed at all but rather surprised that she had come. Plus to find out that they were both Scorpios had seemed special too. And she knew it didn't matter how poor he was. What mattered was that she liked him just the way he was.

Lost in thought, the front door closing got her attention and she pretended to be asleep. She was just tired of being Melvin's housewife, tired of being controlled, tired of being his slave, and just wished she could get Sakena and just haul ass somewhere.

The room light popped on.

She saw it through her eyelids, smelled the alcohol on him. Now he was prowling through the dresser, where she had folded clothes and had ran across his rubbers. He was messing around with somebody. Really wasn't trying to hide it either, not the way he was coming in late and had been acting lately. Probably had been messing around with whoever she was back at his mother's house too. But –

The light faded and she heard the shower running. Thoughts of Pharaoh flooded her mind. Aw... how she wished that it was him taking a shower, him about to come lay down beside her all clean and smelling like Irish Spring. The thought brought about a pleasant smile and she entertained it for a while. But the moment perished ten minutes later when Melvin laid down beside her.

"You up?"

His deep voice was boring to her and she didn't want to move, remaining stiff like the several other times she played asleep until she finally dozed off.

"Monique!"

The getting up out of bed, the flick of the light switch, the sense of his presence standing over her, her eyes still closed, she made no attempt to open them.

"You ain't sleep." His deep voice had a ring to it.

"What do you want?"

Melvin folded his arms, an intense raise of his eyebrows. "I wanna know what's up."

And then her eyes popped opened.

So Melvin hissed and started pacing the room. He was a brown-skinned twenty-three year old, cleaned shaved, chest built. He'd held her locked down for four and a half years. Since he had visited relatives in Ft. Myers and had first tricked with her when she was fifteen. He had brought her to his mother's house after she had told him of her abuse. And there they'd lived and she had gotten pregnant. And now their daughter was going on four.

Monique sighed, "What is it now Melvin?"

"I'm the only one that's trying to make this shit work!"

Monique propped herself up on an elbow saying, "And it don't take no rocket scientist to figure out this shit ain't working."

Melvin stopped pacing and turned around, his look fierce as he scolded her from the foot of the bed. "That's because you don't want this shit to work," he told her, "You keep this lil' funky ass attitude up and I'm gon' keep my daughter. You can take your ass back to Ft. Myers or somewhere. Another bitch gon' be up in here."

Monique sat up quickly. He'd kicked her ass many times but she was going all out about her daughter. "Is you crazy!" she yelled, "I held her in my stomach for nine damn months! I was in labor for seventeen fuckin' hours! You must be done bumped your damn head on something, thinking you just gonna take my daughter away from me. You got life fucked up Melvin!"

His sudden steps made Monique scream and she balled up for the lick.

"You gon' tighten your ass up or get your ass out. I will have my daughter."

"No you want," she fired back, feeling the stinging of her ear. Tears built in the wells of her eyes, and she hatefully stared at him.

Melvin folded his arms. "And what you gon' do?"

Monique jumped up. "I'm sleeping on the sofa." She snatched the blanket and rushed passed him, flinching from just the look in his eyes.

"You ain't nothing but uh ol' bitch anyway, look at'cha… you ain't got shit"!

Monique grabbed her daughter out of her room and settled on the sofa with her. Then, seconds later, she saw him coming.

"Come on now."

Melvin poked her in the side of her face, "Bitch! Keep tryin' me." He walked off.

And so when the room light disappeared Monique sat in the dark having troubled thoughts. However, she closed her eyes while clutching her daughter, until she finally dozed off thinking about Pharaoh.

CHAPTER 3

It was 4am Tuesday morning. Pharaoh was on his way back to the projects in a truck he had rented from a crack-head. No license but he didn't give a damn. He had already broken into two cars. Straight busted the window out of one and had found a chrome .25. He had taken a nice looking Kenwood CD player out of the other one. He didn't care. As long as he saw dollar signs he took the chance.

The streets were vacant. Light poles and traffic lights, night time in the city.

Shit … got dis pistol. Been done robbed me uh store. Yeah! They done fucked up now. Uh po' nigga wit' uh pistol.

Headlights appeared at the light of NE 23rd Avenue and Main, and as Pharaoh slowed into a right, he noticed the red Malibu.

He turned the corner with his eyes hard in the rearview mirror. Where was the baldheaded man going this time of morning strange as Monique had been on his mind lately? Though he hadn't seen her since their last conversation, he somehow felt that he was wrong and should've handled it in a different way. But money was on his mind and since then he had come up to around four hundred dollars.

And so the thought stayed with him as he pulled into Village Green. He was wondering, then, the sight of the fiend coming up the sidewalk made him speed up and stop.

A boy was crossing the median to Forest Green, looking back at them.

"Bet dat up," Pharaoh told her, and hopped out of her red Toyota. His elbow hit the side of the door and he squinched from the pain.

"Anytime," said the fiend, "But do something for me baby. I ain't got nothing but eight."

Pharaoh gave her a nice piece. After all, hadn't he seen her come through the other day – short hair, scars in her face, dingy, but not dirty. Plus she had made the offer when he'd approached the truck, a quarter-piece to rent it for an hour.

"Oh, this is uh nice piece," she marveled, "I need to start coming to see you."

"I be out here all da time."

The truck left and Pharaoh made his way to the back, pants sagging from the small pistol, CD player in hand. When he rounded the building he wasn't surprised to find them both up. They were on front street, right at the stairs.

Richie glanced up. "Toothpick, what's dat ya got?"

"It damn showl ain't no steak Richie. I know you hungry but you can't eat this dawg."

When Pharaoh stopped, Draco browsed over what he held. And Richie continued to cut up crack, leaning against the stairs.

"Let me check dat out," Draco said, and grabbed it from him, "You licked fo' dis?"

"Hell yeah, where else uh po' nigga gonna get it from?" He reached in his pocket, "Licked for dis too."

Richie froze, cookie in hand. "Lemme see dat."

"Ain't nothin' but uh twenty-five"!

Richie sat the cookie on the second step and looked at Pharaoh like he was stupid. "I know pistols."

"Oh, I just didn't want you to think it was food or something."

Draco started laughing.

And Richie snapped, "What da fuck you laughin' at cuz? Dat shit wasn't funny."

Draco hissed under his breath, but he stopped laughing.

And then Richie turned his attention to Pharaoh, "Ya lil' toothpick ass nigga, fuck you!" He snatched the pistol from him, "Lil' boney ass."

Laughing, knowing he'd got in a good one, Pharaoh watched the two cousins check out his stolen merchandise.

"What'cha won't for dis?" Draco asked. "I can put dis in auntie Regal."

"Don't put dat thing in dat raggedy car cuz."

"Why not"? Draco checked it out some more, afterwards lighting a blunt saying, "I'll give ya thirty for it."

"Give it here." Pharaoh rubbed his chin. "In dope though, uh good deal too."

"Alright, alright, I got'cha," He sat the CD player on the bottom step and picked up the cookie.

Richie eyed him. "Don't fuck it up cuz," he hinted. Then he began studying the pistol, turning it from one side to the other.

"I'll give you thirty for dis."

"Nope, ain't for sale," Pharaoh told him.

"Forty."

"Nope"!

After a car crept by, Draco gave him the dope.

Richie said, "Forty-five."

"Ain't selling it"!

"Fifty."

"Alright, now I might shake somethin' for dat."

Richie studied him. He sat the pistol on the bottom step. "Let me count my money 'cause yo' ass think you slick."

Pharaoh grinned as Richie started counting money, turning aside as Draco picked up the pistol. Then the sudden explosion had them all jumping. It had scared the shit out of them.

Draco was looking dumbfounded.

"Goddamn cuz!" Richie wailed, and snatched the pistol from him.

"I ain't know da shit was loaded," Draco replied nervously.

Man…

Now Pharaoh's walk up front was quick. Richie had given him fifty for it. But he got up there and studied the cars in the parking lot. He didn't see the red Malibu. Feeling uneasy, he drifted up the walkway, doubting he should do it. Then he stared around. Windows were dark. No one was out. And feeling the need, he drifted on down to her door, still uncertain. A few seconds later, he knocked, then, seconds after that, the curtains moved.

Stuck, knowing Melvin had just left, and knowing that she had dozed back off after the door had closed. Is it him? Monique thought she was dreaming at first. But with Sakena laying on her, sleeping, breathing, she knew it was reality.

She was up in no time, unlocking the door and snatching him in.

"Damn…" The door closed and he could barely see her. "I just saw ya –."

"Shh…" Grabbing his hand, she pulled him into the room. She was hysterical, amazed that he had come. She went and brushed her teeth and gathered herself together quick. And it took her only seconds to explain that Melvin worked construction and had to be at some jobs early. She then pushed Pharaoh on the bed and hopped on top of him, fumbling to take his belt a-loose.

"Slow down."

"Just hush!"

Rushing, she got his belt a-loose and began tangling with the button. She quickly unfastened it, hearing the un-rippling of the zipper.

"Why you…?"

"Just hush Pharaoh! Hush!"

Pharaoh laid back. Before long, she was sliding down on it, panties brushing the side of his manhood.

"Oh yes, yes…" she whispered, riding him with pleasure.

And so Monique got wild and after ten minutes they were both naked. Pharaoh was captured by the excitement and caught up in the wildness. Kissing, hugging, and touching had both of them twining.

On top, Pharaoh pounded inside of her, feeling the urge of his second one coming along.

"Beat it! Get this pussy! Get this pussy! This your pussy!" Monique sung to him as she moaned and excitedly rubbed his back.

"I can't go no mo'," he said after cumming. Breathing heavy, he fought against collapsing on her.

"Lay down." She pushed up in his chest and was soon on top again, bouncing on it. But after seconds, she felt another one coming and speeded up. She had been lost count at four. Then after it came she decided it was time for a break. She got up and hit the light switch, smiling as she stared at him.

Pharaoh sat up.

"No," Monique spoke more with both hands, "No, just stay there, you hungry, you thirsty"?

"No."

"I got orange juice, grape juice, cranberry juice -."

"You trippin,"

"You gotta use the bathroom?"

"Naw…"

"Okay, just stay there. I'm gonna bring you something back anyways."

When she disappeared Pharaoh snapped out of the quick trance. It was a plain room – big bed, dresser with a TV on it. On top of the nightstand were a cordless phone, radio, and an alarm clock. A hair bag was in the corner sitting underneath a tall lamp. The more he lay there the more he became uncomfortable. Then she came back, glowing with a big white cup and a big bag of Doritos.

Naked, Monique sat on the edge of the bed and handed him the cup. There was a big wet spot in the middle and she knew exactly what she had to do.

"What's this?"

"Grape juice," She glared back at him, "What made you come?" With joy in her eyes, she opened the Doritos. "I miss you. I'm so glad to see you."

It was this moment that Pharaoh finally decided to say, "I see. But what's really going on wit' you?"

Astonished, Monique sat a hand on his leg. "Do you really wanna know Pharaoh?" As she made sense of his peculiar look, she glanced at the clock. It was 4:46am. "He's gonna be back around three today." Thinking and knowing that she couldn't let her daughter see Pharaoh, she got up and closed the room door. Then she cuddled up beside him.

CHAPTER 4

Now the early morning was filled with mysterious and unusual emotions. Monique had fallen dead silent now. She had told Pharaoh about Ft Myers and growing up with her alcoholic father. But he had asked her what had made her come to Gainesville. So, still, she hadn't responded, laying in his arms and gazing at the wall, solemn-like.

"What's wrong, talk?" he said softly, brushing her hair back as she gazed at him, "Oh… you got amnesia or somethin' now. Shit… I don't, my momma uh crack-head and she smoke dope like, man…"

"You crazy"! She giggled.

"Okay, see ya laughin' now."

"'Cause you crazy Pharaoh," she insisted with a spirited grin.

"Okay, since you say I'm crazy, I'm crazy. But om… back to you. Ya daddy was uh alcoholic and ya'll use to fight a lot, but where Gainesville come in the picture at? And where ya momma was?"

"My momma died when I was two. I barely even remember her."

Silence lasted for every bit of ten seconds before Pharaoh lowered his eyes at her.

"Okay," she said, "You ain't gotta look crazy like that."

"I'm listenin'."

"We got in a big fight one day," she paused, smiling as his hand started rubbing her butt, "My daddy was real drunk and I knocked over his bottle."

"Whoa… you mean to tell me dat you knocked over a liquor drinker's bottle."

"It's not funny," she said seriously, but couldn't help grinning at his giggles, "Stop laughing Pharaoh, it's not funny. He left it in the bathroom and I had to pee real bad… It was dark." When he laughed harder she smiled at him and rolled on top of him. "Stop laughing." She kissed him when he didn't. Then, lightly biting his bottom lip, she told him, "It's not funny. I ran away from home with a swollen jaw and a black eye."

"You ran away from home?"

"Yep"!

Their silence was eye locking. While Pharaoh was stuck, dazed about it, Monique was stuck trying to read his reaction. However, eye contact was broken when she softly kissed his chest.

"I just couldn't take the shit no more."

"So you came to Gainesville?"

"After I ran into Melvin that night and he saw my face after –." She dropped her chin in his chest.

"After what?" he asked curiously.

For several seconds, Monique just gazed at the wall, "I don't think this is a good time for me –."

"Why not"? "

"He followed me for two blocks down Martin Luther King offering me forty dollars!" she blurted crazily, "It was three o'clock in the morning Pharaoh!"

"And"!

"Pharaoh"!

"And"!

"And I finally stopped and got in. And he saw my face. I was only fifteen Pharaoh!"

"Did you tell him what happened?"

"Yeah," she said softly, "I told him."

Pharaoh lowered his eyes at her, clearly imagining everything she was telling him. "Go 'head."

Monique sighed and took a deep breath, "He gave me the money and we got in the back seat." After she glanced at him and saw that it didn't affect him, she was a little startled. "After that," she said, "We talked. He told me he was visiting relatives and was on his way back home. And he asked me did I wanna come." She thought a second and whined crazily, "I wasn't going back home Pharaoh. I thought my jaw was fractured and my eye was really, really bad."

"So you came to Gainesville?"

"Yep, with him to his momma's house,"

"His momma house," he stated weirdly.

"Yep, out by the mall, on fifty-fifth."

"And his momma didn't say shit about it?"

"Tina had a lot of shit to say about it. She took me back to Ft. Myers the next day. But when we got there my daddy was real drunk and acting real stupid. He cursed me and her out, called us bitches and everything."

"Damn…"

"Yep, and I think that's when she changed her mind, because I was going in the house and she just told me to get my stuff and come on." She planted a kiss on his lips, breaking his daze. "My life real crazy Pharaoh, I can't believe I'm telling you this shit."

"So you came back with her," he stated interestingly, running his fingers through her long hair. He stared at her titties for a brief moment then swung his gaze back into her hazel eyes.

"I had my own room and stuff. It took about three months for her to really loosen up. But by that time I was already pregnant with Sakena."

"His momma let'chall get down like dat?"

"Pharaoh, this is crazy," she whined.

"For real"!

"No and yeah," she replied uncomfortably, "After I started showing real bad she just kinda let things go and I started sleeping in the room with him. It was crazy."

"What?"

Monique sighed. "Everything, after the baby, school, and I kinda wanna own my own hair salon Pharaoh. I can do hair real good. I had to get my GED after I got pregnant again."

"Where ya other shorty"?

"I had a miscarriage," she said sadly, "…All the arguing, fighting, I got my license and still couldn't go nowhere."

"Couldn't go nowhere,"

"Yeah, he wants me to be like his damn momma. She's uh fucking housewife Pharaoh. She doesn't do shit, and always wanted me to fix her hair up good so she can show off in church."

Pharaoh giggled, "Show off in church wit' uh hair-do."

Monique sat up. "I'm really good. My dad had this girlfriend once when I was thirteen. I really liked her. Her name was Brenda. She was a hairstylist Pharaoh. She taught me everything." Her tone died. "Before my daddy started beating on her. I woke up one morning and she was just gone." The nightstand was in arms reach. She grabbed the Doritos, ate one, and fed him one. Then she decided to tell him, "Melvin's mom got pissed when I didn't feel like doing her hair one morning. He got pissed because she was mad at me and hit me. So I did it, and I started to make her hair fall out too."

He laughed.

"I'm for real though Pharaoh." She took a long breath as she lied back on top of him, saying, "You just don't understand."

"Why ya sayin' it like dat?"

"Well, his father died and supposedly used to take care of them. Melvin still helps her pay her bills even though we're out here now, and swears he's saving money to move us to a better place, although I don't know how." Suddenly, she looked into his eyes. The thought had instantly occurred to her. So she reached down and pinched him between the thighs.

"Owh…" He grabbed her and flipped her over. "What was that for?"

"Cause I haven't fucked him for real in two months. He's reminding me of my damn daddy."

"Ya daddy,"

"He drinks Pharaoh and he's putting his hands on me a lot. His momma got tired of us so we're out here now. And I feel like I'm trapped."

Now by the time dawn illuminated the bedroom window, Monique was cooking breakfast for him. And Pharaoh knew he hated Melvin but understood that it wasn't his problem. Or was it? They ate at seven — cheese grits, bacon, eggs, and toast. Then they went at it again. But by eight, she was stressing that her daughter would be up soon and explained to him that he had to go.

Thinking, watching him getting dressed, wishing he could stay, feeling hopeless, Monique began scrambling through a dresser drawer; knowing Melvin wouldn't miss it. "You gotta put minutes on it now."

It was a little gray Nokia, and before Pharaoh knew it, she was plundering through the closet and pulling out the adapter for it. "You trippin'."

"No I'm not and don't say that." She walked up to him. "I wanna be able to talk to you Pharaoh. It's mine and I don't even use it," They kissed and she slipped on something, walking him to the door. Sakena was still asleep, "Put minutes on it now."

"I will," His eyes browsed the sofa. He could barely see her daughter's hair, "Do she look like you?"

Monique smiled. "A little bit. Now go before she wakes up."

And so Pharaoh kissed Monique before he stepped out to find Peanut running up the walkway. Peanut was a bad little eight- year old who was always getting into something.

Peanut slowed down when he saw Pharaoh and started giggling. "Dat ain't your house."

"Peanut!" Pharaoh said through clenched teeth, "Take ya lil' bad ass… on somewhere."

"Still ain't your house."

Tired, Pharaoh made his way upstairs, underminding the few people that saw him leaving there. After plugging the adapter in the wall to charge the cell phone, he took a shower to get the arousing scent of Monique off of him. Finally, he flopped down on his mattress; drained, thinking it would be easy to relax. But with her cell phone and just knowing of her troubles, he closed his eyes and found it hard to go to sleep.

When loud bangs struck the door an hour later, Pharaoh sluggishly got up, knowing only one person knocked on his door like that, he opened it saying, "What momma?"

"I need ten dollars Pharaoh," *I knew my baby was home.* Rose came in and closed the door behind her, smiling as her son started walking away. *My baby!* "I'll give it back to you later on baby." She followed him to his room. Rose was a short woman, five-three with a sweet voice, and she had been very attractive back in the days when she had worked as Ester Paynes secretary; organizing cases and getting her prepared for court. She had been good. Or like Ester had called her, the one who always kept things organized and ready. But now that beauty was fading and she didn't look half as good as she had a few years ago. Her skin was once this cocoa brown. It seemed dull and extra weary now. Her fraught face was maimed from years of smoking, cheekbones sharp and eyes sunken. Black pouches hung underneath them like water, swollen from days of no sleeping. Her hair was short and kinked up. Her clothes seemed to swallow her. She was wearing dingy jeans, a faded gray shirt, and worn out brown sandals. Rose now stopped in his doorway and sat her hands on her boney hips, chewing on her jaw as he paused to look at her. *Don't start!* She eyed him.

"Momma, you don't ever gimme my money back." He picked up his pants and went in his pocket.

"I will today baby. Ya momma gotta job. That's why you haven't been seeing me."

Yeah right momma, uh job smoking crack! He gave her a twenty dollar bill, thinking she was probably going to Richie. He thought about giving her dope but it was no way that he could bring himself to doing that.

"Thank you baby," She kissed him. *My Pharaoh!*

"Mah, you need to leave dat shit alone."

"I'm going to baby, real soon." She hurried off.

Ya tell me da same shit every time ya come momma, Lord have mercy! He flopped on his mattress, thinking; the sound of the door closing barely hitting his ears. He hadn't acted like it, but, he was glad that she had stopped by and happy to know that she was alright. He loved her to death, no matter how bad she was strung out. She had always taken care of him until the problem had gotten too bad.

Closing his eyes, Monique came to mind. Then he finally dozed off thinking about putting minutes on the cell-phone.

CHAPTER 5

Rose scurried on out of Village Green and up the sidewalk of 15th Street. She wasn't going back there to the Big One. She already knew she owed him twenty dollars. She hadn't been back to her apartment in days. And last night Deborah had dropped her off. So she had dodged the Big One last night and this morning, yet, had been sending Deborah to him quite a few times. Now her destination was back Crosstown. Had gotten a little sleep and she would now find Deborah. Maybe Deborah had gotten a little sleep herself, or wide awake for somebody wanting fresh meat.

It was around nine that night when Pharaoh woke up and gathered his thoughts together. He decided to walk to the store, where he bought minutes for the cell-phone and some blunts. He would get a sack from Draco. No sooner as he had been to Draco and was walking back up, the cell-phone rang with a funny tune. He answered to the voice of Monique. Then he heard a deep voice in the background. Suddenly, the other end went dead. *Man...*

A hustler was posted up in the breezeway. A few people were scattered about. He rolled a blunt and happened to catch a swing. By now, it seemed the police had started riding. Later that night, he was in his apartment when the funny tunes played again. It was Monique asking him where he was and telling him that she was coming up there.

Pharaoh shook his head. And it was a few minutes later that he opened the door saying, "You trippin' hard…"

"No I'm not," She was glowing to find him wearing nothing but boxers. After closing the door, she turned around and simply bent over. She was wearing nothing under that long black shirt, "Hurry up!"

Pharaoh didn't hesitate and reacted off of impulse. Once he was inside of her he was lost in the thrill of the moment. From the front door to the living room floor, from there to his single mattress, Monique started squirting like crazy. He was tearing that pussy up.

"Uh…uh… Pharaoh," Her lips were on his neck, her legs were wrapped around his back. Her mouth was open. She was gasping. It felt so good she started crying. Passion! He came inside her. They lay breathless. And she felt the pulsing between her legs. "Oh my God Pharaoh!" she cried, "I really hope you know what you doing."

"What'cha mean?" His lips were touching hers. "Cause you just cummin' all in me."

Soon, she trotted back down the steps and eased the door open. Melvin was still asleep and Sakena was the same way she had left her.

Richie stepped out of his auntie's door, "Cuz"!

Draco was talking to a girl, "What?"

"You out here doin' all dat goddamn talkin' and them nigga's ain't came back wit' dat money yet."

"They gon' come."

"Fuck dat," Richie snapped, "Told your stupid ass not to front dem nigga's. You ain't learnt shit yet, shorta than uh motherfucka fuckin' wit' you. Need to go find somethin' 'cause we 'bout out, and you ain't finna fuck up no mo' either."

Draco hissed, "Ain't my fault."

"Yeah it is," Richie mean mugged him, "You don't know how to sell dope nigga, 'round here tryin' to front."

Now Crosstown was Rose's stumping grounds. This had been her area of comfort every since she had started smoking, and Deborah was a new face around there who'd moved from God knows where. Deborah had told her that she was from Williston. On the other hand, Rose was use to people lying. She had heard it all and seen it all in the streets. But she hadn't known that Deborah's nephew was Lake Road Slim though. He was a well known one from the side of the Lake Road projects that sat off of East University.

The old lady that Deborah had moved in with had always rented rooms out, and, if Deborah was telling the truth about how her old man smoked and had done her, Rose could certainly identify with that feeling. When she had first started smoking it had been the same with her – getting pimped around, dope boy to dope boy. She had been something to get at back then. But the only difference now was that she had lost her car and Deborah still had her truck. And she had lost the house off of NW 8th Avenue, moving to Village Green. But –.

The both of them had ended up at a house a couple blocks over from 5t Avenue, and like usual, it was booming. The house was damn near packed. On the porch was an old smoker who was tapping his foot and looking up and down the street. He would go back in, take a hit, and tell the boys what it looked like out there. From experience, everybody knew what time it was if the police were riding.

A car pulled up and Rose knew the man. She told him to wait and then approached Deborah. She then told Deborah to follow them. They were on the move.

CHAPTER 6

"You think you be doing something, don'tcha?"

"What'cha mean?"

Monique sat up like it was nothing to it. It was a windy afternoon, and her and her daughter had just come back from a short walk to the corner store with him. The little boy Peanut had come along as well. Pharaoh had bought him something too.

"How you think you be having me all folded up," she told him.

"Oh, you don't like it?"

Monique pulled the spread back on the bed, smiling, "I ain't said nothing, you can get it how ya wanna. But you just can't go the distance."

"I bet dat."

She rolled over on her elbows and knees, dropped low and butted it up for him. "Well, what are you stopping for? Put it back in and get busy."

Pharaoh grinned, "Your ass done got loose."

She sat back up and glared at him, "Why, because I walked to the store with you, and you not doing nothing but spoiling her Pharaoh, she probably out there with a big mess." She laid back.

"Good, dat mean you'll have something to do."

Monique smacked her lips. "Pharaoh, that ain't cute. I don't need ice cream and doughnuts everywhere. I'll have to clean it up before Melvin gets here."

He stood. "But you done got loose."

Monique sat up again, browsing over his naked body. "Well, I just did it to see if you had a girlfriend or not."

Pharaoh frowned, looking back at her. "Why da fuck you just didn't ask me?"

"Don't talk to me like that Pharaoh."

"Well, why da fuck you just didn't ask me?"

Monique kept silent.

"And if that red car woulda bent the corner ya ass woulda been running for ya life."

The beat-up green Chevette tipped into Village Green that following afternoon.

Pharaoh was approaching the window of the white Datsun when he seen it.

"You holding?" was Ted's rusty voice.

"What'cha talking 'bout"!

"Just look out for me man," Ted reached in the seat and handed over some balled up money.

After counting sixteen dollars, Pharaoh looked over at Boochie parking. He then gave Ted a piece, told him his name, and told him the cell number.

Ted went to fidgeting. "Just throw me one mo' piece man."

"Damn…" Pharaoh cried, "I gave ya uh juggler."

"Just one more now, I'mma call you, Pharaoh." Ted pointed at him. "Yeah, thought I forgot your name, didn't ya?" He hastily began rambling through the car for a piece of paper and a pencil, where he wrote down Pharaoh's number. Car parts were everywhere on the floorboard.

Pharaoh thought a second. *A baser named Ted.* He gave him his smallest piece. By now, Boochie was out and was approaching.

Ted smiled. He eyed Pharaoh with the light of being satisfied, saying, "I'mma call you now, Pharaoh,"

Boochie walked up.

And the white Datsun pulled into an empty space, backed up, and headed back out.

"What up dawg?"

"Not shit," Pharaoh gave him some dap, "Wanna smoke?"

"Where it at"?

"See, the only time ya wanna bring ya ass back."

Boochie chuckled.

"C'mon, let's ride back here to Draco nigga."

In the back of the projects, the dented up black Buick Regal with no hubcaps had just backed out. Draco was fumbling with the shaft when they rode up. He was trying to get it to go into drive. It finally did.

Pharaoh had already gotten out. To the right, Richie was talking to a boy out there. "What's wrong wit' it?" Pharaoh asked.

"Transmission," Draco spoke to Boochie.

And Richie had already started walking over there. He said, "Oh shit, the two bandits are back together."

Boochie spoke to Richie but that was it. He didn't vibe with Richie at all.

"Toothpick," Richie came with, stopping only feet away from the beat up green Chevette, a smirk on his face, "I heard about'cha lil' boney ass and dat new girl."

Pharaoh turned around to look at him. "I don't know what you talking about." He then turned back around and got the sack from Draco, who was putting a CD in the CD player he had bought from him.

"I'll holler at'cha, I gotta run right quick," said Draco.

Richie told him, "You shoulda been gone already anyways cuz." And then the Regal pulled off.

Pharaoh was getting back in when he saw Richie's look again.

"Yeah, I heard about'cha toothpick." Richie kept nodding his head.

With a straight face, Pharaoh looked in his eyes and told him, "For real, I don't know what you talkin' 'bout."

Richie's face went blank.

And that's all it took for Boochie to pull off. He said, "I see Richie still with that ole bully bullshit, like everybody scared of him."

"Yep, Richie still da same."

"I couldn't be Draco," Boochie shook that big tank head of his, shooting Pharaoh that straight look, "I woulda been done fucked him up."

"Shoulda seen da way he looked at him da other night."

"Who"?

"Draco!" Pharaoh came with, "Shit… shot Richie uh mean unit dawg." He slung his boney arm out the window. "Where we goin'"?

"Get blunts."

They rode and got blunts. Came back and hung out. They'd been road dawgs a long time, since maybe a month after Rose had moved there. The adjustment had been a little rough for Pharaoh, who'd had to adapt to the environment, and at fourteen not use to fighting he quickly had to learn how. Boochie on the other hand had already had a reputation. People knew he fought hard and was down to earth, and didn't like starting anything.

A problem with Richie awhile back had just been words. Pharaoh had been there. It had been over basically nothing, just Richie's big mouth. Draco had been there too. Pharaoh thought it had been about to go down, hoping Draco wouldn't jump in or he would pop him. But it never happened though.

As time passed, Pharaoh told Boochie about Monique. And Boochie just shook his head and told him to be careful. A mention of Kitty's name reminded Pharaoh how scheming some could be. Kitty had led him to believe that he was the only one. Later he found out he was just one of many. She didn't stay out there with her sister anymore. But on some occasions he did see her.

The screams of a baby being put in a car seat drew no attention. The sun was setting. Across the street in front of Rawlings Elementary, a couple was arguing and making a big scene.

"It's getting late."

"Yeah, I know what dat mean, Michelle."

"You still on dat,"

Pharaoh looked at him, "How can I not be dawg, just hauled ass on uh nigga?"

"Well," Boochie gazed three spaces down at the red Malibu, "From what I see, it seems like you done stuck ya hands in some shit."

"I hate dat nigga dawg."

In disbelief, Boochie came with, "You don't even much know dat man. Don't know if that girl done filled your head up wit' some shit or not. See how Kitty did ya."

"But this shit different."

"And what make you think that?"

Pharaoh folded his arms. "'Cause I just know dawg, I feel it."

Boochie shook his head again. "Man… I finna go"!

"I know it."

"I'll come holler at'cha tomorrow dawg."

"Yeah right, tomorrow to you mean next week sometime."

"I'm for real," Boochie insisted, "Gotta go somewhere first, but I'll be here about five." He began staring around Village Green, then Forest Green, as if reminiscing on his past years.

Pharaoh doubted he would see him but said anyways, "I'll have some weed for ya dawg."

CHAPTER 7

It turned out to be a pretty good morning for Pharaoh. Monique and Sakena were mostly with him. By noon he walked to Richie and found out that Richie was out of dope. Too hot out there, he went to her apartment and hung out. But later on they were back out there.

A short while later, Pharaoh seen the red truck bend the corner. Just before it got to him, he gazed down to see the dented up black Buick Regal following. He could tell Richie was in the passenger's seat.

"Hey baby," the fiend said, "You do be out here, don'tcha?"

"Yeah," He stepped to the window, "What's up?"

"Oh, nothing, I just want you to do something good for these thirty dollars I got."

It was his last two jugglers, and he didn't see Richie's gesture when he sold it to her.

After the red truck left, the dented up black Buick Regal came to a halt with screeching breaks and a light odor of gas fumes reeking from it. Richie had a wod of cash in his lap and Draco was behind the wheel with a freshly lit blunt.

"Goin' to pick dat up," Richie said, "Where ya lil' boney ass gon' be?"

"I'll be 'round here."

Monique was in the breezeway when he came back, her white sundress looking good on her. Her hair was in a fancy up-do, and Sakena's hair was in two perfect ponytails.

"This all you ever do all day?"

"Pretty much,"

"You don't think you gonna get caught?"

Pharaoh looked at her. "Man… it is what it is."

Monique bit her bottom lip. "Well, I see more in you than that."

He stepped back. "Well, tell me what you see in me."

She smiled. "I see a nice person with a kind heart –."

"Who po', ain't got shit, and strugglin'."

They talked for minutes, and for a while. Then, after Pharaoh bought Sakena a freeze cup, they heard his named being called.

"Richie said c'mon," Draco told him and disappeared around the corner.

Monique took the freeze cup from Sakena. "I'm gonna let her finish eating it, don't look at me like that boy."

"Ya bedda"!

"Gone ahead and handle ya business. I'll call ya later on."

Pharaoh grabbed her and pulled her close. "But you ain't gave me them panties you owe me yet,"

"You want me to take them off now." She glanced around, and then she lifted her sundress a little at the side, posing for him. "And they your favorite color too."

"How you know blue my favorite color?"

"Well, I assume that because that's what color most of your boxers got in it," She smiled, and was biting her bottom lip with a grin just before walking off, "Now am I close or did I hit it on the head." She looked back at him. "Call you later on."

Pharaoh just stared at her before he made his way out front, where Draco was getting in the driver's seat and Richie's fat elbow hung out the window. Then all in one motion he broke stride. Melvin walked right pass him. But he continued, assuming Monique and Sakena would already be inside of their apartment.

…Monique was just stepping in when she heard his voice and jerked her body to the left to see him.

"What da fuck is you doin"?

She pushed Sakena inside and told her to go to her room. With the freeze cup in her hand, she backed up and began to get her story together.

The door flew open all the way and slammed back. Melvin stood there with concrete on his boots and clothes, eyes burning with rage.

"What da fuck is you doing?"

"I just went to get Sakena uh freeze –."

"Dressed like that!"

Monique balled up for it but the lick tossed her sideways, knocking the freeze cup on the carpet, where some splashed along the wall.

"Stop it Melvin!"

The loud cry of Sakena pierced the apartment. She heard the smacking sounds and though she couldn't see she knew exactly what was going on.

"Melvin, stop!" Monique gurgled from the pressure of being choked, digging her nails deep in his face and skin. Then, she was slapped hard and knocked to the floor.

"I'll kill you bitch!"

"Stop it Melvin!" Monique screamed, feeling the pain of her jaw and lips. She tried to fight him off but she knew she was no match. After she was slapped in the face again and thrown on the sofa, she screamed at the top of her lungs and balled up in pain. When she was yanked up by her hair and slung, she crashed into the wall, screaming, "Melvin, stop!"

"And got my daughter walkin' around out here," He stormed to Sakena's room and got her.

"Top daddy," Sakena cried, wiggling in his grasp, "Mommy!"

When the door closed Monique could barely get up. A trickle of blood ran out of the corner of her mouth and she opened the door, dizzy. "Gimme my baby Melvin," she screamed, ignoring the stares of several people, "Pharaoh, Pharaoh!" she screamed as she ran.

…And so Pharaoh was staring at the dope in Richie's hand when he heard his name being screamed. When he saw Sakena crying and Melvin carrying her to the car, he knew something had gone down. He eyed Melvin evil-like, hearing the cries of Monique. Then she bent the corner, running, and the sight of seeing her hit him hard. Her hair was wild and the second thing he noticed was blood on her white sundress.

"Pharaoh, he trying to take my baby," Monique screamed, rushing to the car, where Melvin was putting Sakena in the front seat, "No, gimme my baby"!

Melvin slammed the door and started walking towards her, pointing his finger at her, making her back away. "Bitch"!

Richie and Draco sat stunned, glued into the whole thing.

"Dat dude finna fuck her up cuz!" Richie said, holding a whole cookie of crack. When he saw Pharaoh dart across in front of the car, he slowly pulled the latch. "What Pharaoh finna do?"

"I told'cha they said Pharaoh was fuckin' dat girl. I just seen him talking to her."

"Oh…shit!" Richie sat the cookie on the dashboard and got out. Pharaoh rushed and grabbed Monique. He yanked her behind him just before Melvin could get his hands on her.

"What nigga?"

"My baby Pharaoh, get my baby!" Monique was crying and beating on his shoulders. She saw how Sakena was crying and beating on the window. She struck out to the other side of the car.

"Bitch"! Melvin shot back around and chased her back around the car, while his eyes slashed to the skinny fellow that she was calling Pharaoh. He shouted, "What nigga?"

Angry, Pharaoh stepped off the sidewalk. He couldn't believe Monique's face until she scuffled to get around him.

"Pharaoh, what you think you gon' do nigga?"

No…. Not between these cars. Swinging his elbows back, tapping Monique, Pharaoh started backing up.

Richie and Draco stood and watched as people began to gather around.

"Pharaoh don't act like he wanna do nothin', Draco stated weirdly, "Dat nigga gotta lil' size too"!

Richie began wondering when Pharaoh backed off the sidewalk. But when he saw him stop, he folded his fat arms and said, "Oh, Pharaoh finna bump!"

"Yeah he is"!

Melvin had both of his fists clenched, raging and swinging his arms. "What nigga? What'cha wanna do?" He was hollering, "What, you act like you wanna do somethin', act like you fuckin' her or somethin' nigga!"

"I am fuckin' her and what you gon' do 'bout it nigga," Pharaoh fired back, squaring off and moving, "What I know is you ain't gon' put'cha hands on her no more and Sakena coming up out dat car."

"What?" Stunned by the sting of his daughter's name, Melvin peered at Monique with rising rage.

"Showl is fucking him Melvin. Why you think I've been sleeping on the sofa? That's because I've been fucking him."

The rage of Melvin was explosive. Pharaoh stepped aside and popped off. But somehow Melvin grabbed him and slung him. He ended up back in front of the red Malibu, where he was snatched up like a piece of paper and all he seen was sky. Thundered quaked with impact the moment he crashed down on the hood of the red Malibu – a jolt of lightning shooting up his back. But he managed to kick Melvin in the face and roll off of the hood, fleeing in the open road for more room and enough time to get his wind back.

It was a man that ran from around the building hollering, "Somebody stop'em!"

By now Melvin had met Pharaoh with vicious blows. But Pharaoh was sticking and moving. He had hands. The only thing that mattered to him was don't let Melvin grab him again. He was popping off, and a leaky cut was just above Melvin's left eye. Following that was a growing lump on the right side of Melvin's forehead.

And then the beat up green Chevette whipped in.

And Richie got excited. He saw how quick Boochie suddenly hopped out, so he scrambled to the side of the Regal. He pulled it out but it was too late. Boochie had laid one solid lick. The man was down. And Richie, pointing the pistol at the dazed man who was trying to get up, started walking towards him thundering words.

CHAPTER 8

Things had died down over the next few minutes. The red Malibu was gone with the dent crinched in the hood where Pharaoh had been slammed. The crowd had thinned out a bit.

And Richie was hyped up. He told Pharaoh, "C'mon nigga. You want dis, don'tcha."

"Hell yeah, I spent my money, didn't I?"

Boochie watched the transaction and scolded Richie at the same time. Upon Pharaoh's return, he said, "I don't know why you mess wit' them."

"Man… I gotta go see about this girl."

They started around the building, where Peanut had been at the corner watching.

"She stand'n by your house Pharaoh," Peanut told him, "Cry'n and hold'n her baby."

Upstairs, Monique was shaking and holding her daughter tight with tear lines running down both sides of her swollen face. She looked at Pharaoh with quivering lips and nervously asked, "Where he at?"

"He gone,"

"Something's gonna happened to us Pharaoh," she suddenly cried out, "Please don't let nothing happen."

They went in his apartment and Boochie hung back. Monique was scared to death and Pharaoh leaned on the wall, still holding the dope. The swelling on her face had increased and her puffy lip had gotten bigger. He could see the smeared blood where she had wiped it off with her shoulder. The cut was small but it looked awful whenever her lips quivered to say something, while Sakena sniffled with both arms around her, tears falling from her innocent eyes.

"Ya'll can stay here but," He looked around, "I ain't really got nothin'."

"We can't go back down there Pharaoh," Monique grieved horribly, "He's gonna come back and something's going to happen to us. Please Pharaoh. Don't let nothing happen to me and my baby."

"Ain't nothin' gon' happen to ya'll." Pharaoh knew he wasn't going to let Melvin hurt her again. And just spending with Richie had him almost broke with ninety-two dollars in his pocket, but, eyeing the dope in his hand with the thought its money, then gazing into Monique's hazel eyes, he peered at Sakena with a sad feeling, wondering what Melvin might do. "Jus' chill and stay here." He kissed her, and then stepped out.

The balcony wasn't empty at all. It seemed like everybody was out there. Below, glances from the people probably still talking about it.

Boochie was paying attention to his right hand. It appeared that he'd pushed back a knuckle. He asked Pharaoh where the weed was and got pissed when he heard Draco's name. So he fired off, cursing under his breath.

Inside, the bathroom mirror reflected an awful sight as Monique cleaned herself up. Pharaoh made sure she was alright before he went in his room, grabbing a razor and drawing careful lines on the cookie. What was he going to do when Melvin came back? He really didn't know. But by the time he filled up his Tylenol bottle he knew that he would find a way.

A slight knock was confusing a few seconds later and Pharaoh paused, staring at the remainder of the pieces that he was considering where to hide at.

"Oh my God, it's him, Pharaoh!" Monique flew out of the bathroom, holding Sakena.

"It's Boochie."

A sigh of relief filled her when he opened the door and she saw the boy who'd came up with him, but, when he stepped outside, her heart raced. "Where you going"?

"Don't worry. I'll be right out here." He left the door open so she could see him and told Boochie how it started.

All the while they talked and smoked, Boochie was telling him how Richie and Draco had been back there acting.

"Man, you need to leave dem nigga's alone."

"Ain't nothin' but uh dope thing dawg."

"That's you," Boochie hissed, "Glad I'm out dis shit."

"Yeah, bet you are."

Boochie passed him the blunt saying, "I ain't mean it like dat."

At that instance two of the girls passed. One was Vickie – a big boned, jazzy red with four gold teeth. She said, "Ugh, well stand up in da paint then Pharaoh."

Pharaoh looked at her. "Whatever."

"Cause you fight for who you wanna be with 'round here, huh?"

"Girl gone"!

"And I know dat's right." The two girls fell into laughter.

Boochie turned to him. "Your ass gon' fuck around and be in jail or the graveyard."

Pharaoh eyed him seriously. "Whatever. Then gon' back to ya girl you done ran off wit', cause you liable to die or go to jail fuckin' wit me. I don't want nobody to say, Boochie got fucked up fuckin' wit' Pharaoh." He was heated and went back in.

A slight breeze was blowing at 10 that night when Pharaoh walked them down there to get clothes and stuff. The phone was ringing off the hook, and Monique knew it was Melvin or either Tina. Because his back was hurting, while she was telling Sakena to get all of her toys and stuff, he stretched out on the floor and went to gazing at the ceiling. It wasn't long before he realized that she was packing food too. Bags were by the sofa in the living room. And everything was quiet when loud bangs struck the door.

Gasping, Monique snatched the curtains back and let out a long whiff of air. Relieved, she smiled at the fiend. "You got a customer. It's uh lady."

"Dat ain't no customer."

"Yes it is, she looking at me real real crazy and she biting on her jaw."

"Open the door. Dat's my momma."

Feeling ashamed, Monique let her in. She then opened the bag of fruit snacks for Sakena, stopping her daughter's whines. When she realized his mother's eyes were on her, she studied her like a little girl.

Rose stood there in her dingy blue jeans, faded black shirt, and worn out brown sandals. Black pouches hung underneath both her eyes and her kinked up hair was partially combed, yet the look in her wide eyes was baffling and she sat that hand on her hip. "That boy did that to you," she yelped.

Spiritless, Monique softly said, "Yes ma'am."

"And you ain't cut him?" Rose stood there and waited for a response, but she didn't get one. *Huh!* "What's ya name?"

"Monique."

"And what's ya daughter name?"

"Sakena."

Rose squinted her eyes. "You love my son?"

"Yes, yes ma'am." Monique was ashamed a little. But her mind automatically insinuated a performance on his mother's hair. A good combing, a good washing, a good perm, and she could work a miracle with the length. It wasn't that long.

Rose eyed her son down there and walked on over, staring down at him. "Boy, is you alright? They say you got slammed pretty hard."

"I'm alright mah. What'cha need?"

Rose scratched the side of her head. "Well, I came to see if you were alright," she said truthfully. The boys had told her that he was down there, "But since you asked me, can you stand… twenty dollars." She grinned when he went in his pocket. *My baby!* "And I see you and Linda nephews stick together now, say the Big One ran him off with a pistol, they something else now she in jail." She grabbed the money from him and stuck it in her bra. "Whelp, you alright, let me get to going. Got my friend out there waiting on me," On her way out, she passed Monique saying, "And child… I woulda cut the shit out of his ass and kept cutting, cause Rose don't play dat shit,"

Monique somehow sensed a warm feeling about Rose. And ten minutes later they were back up there in Pharaoh's apartment. She hadn't known that Melvin had had a pistol pulled on him. Maybe that was good. But she was thinking why she hadn't cut him just like Rose had said.

CHAPTER 9

The following day was shaky but there was a no show from Melvin. And by eight that evening Monique was in Pharaoh's kitchen throwing down – pork chops, yellow rice, black eyed peas, cornbread muffins.

With a sore back, Pharaoh hadn't done too much of nothing and hadn't been anywhere at all, except downstairs to see if Melvin's car was back and to take Monique in there to get pots and pans. He had found Sakena playful when he'd grabbed one of her Barbie dolls. The only explanation he had for Melvin not coming back: perhaps Richie had put the fear of God in him.

"She not yike dem ones Pairoh," Sakena said, and picked up the other one, "Her do."

"That one"!

"Uh-huh. She name Barbie Pairoh."

Monique strolled out there to watch them. Her face was so awful. It would take awhile for the swelling to leave. This was the worst it had ever been, "Are ya'll having fun down there?"

Sakena sparkled, "Me an Pairoh pay wit me Barbie dolls mommy, tee." Sakena showed her one of the three she had that they were putting clothes on.

Monique glowed at Pharaoh and was just about to comment when the cell-phone rung and changed her feelings. Impulsively, she stared at it on the floor beside him and got scared when he answered it.

Baser Ted's voice sounded even rustier on the phone to Pharaoh. After he told her everything was alright, he told him where to find him.

When the knock came they were eating, and he slowly got up and stepped outside.

Ted started sniffing. "Boy, them smell like pork chops in there," He sniffed again, "Uh-hu, pork chops."

Pharaoh giggled. "What up?"

"Fifty man, fifty," Ted told him, and handed him the money with a perky look, "Ya might have to leave wit' me later on."

"I ain't goin' nowhere,"

"No, no, no," he said, grabbing the pieces, "Like what ya did for me the other day. See," he began explaining, "I got this crack'h in uh room. He be trickin'. Be spending all time of night," he went into saying, more like whispering to him, "Fifty's, hundreds. I done seen one night where he spent five."

"Oh yeah"!

"Yeah man," Ted nodded and crankily added, "Only thing about it is he go to actin' crazy."

Pharaoh folded his arms. "What'cha mean?"

Ted gestured with a stupefied pull on his crotch. "Crack'h crazy," he told him, "Get real high and don't want nobody to leave the room. And I know he gon' send me back for more, so ya might have to end up coming with me, he spend."

Pharaoh said, "Shit... call me before ya come."

The call came an hour later. Monique was massaging his lower back. After he told her what to do and what the deal was, he got dressed and stepped out.

And so the white Datsun soon showed up and Pharaoh was off for the first time with Baser Ted. The ride to the Knights Inn didn't take too long. It was just like Ted had said. But it wasn't even two hours later that he had to get him to bring him back for more. He swore he would've brought it all if he had known it would be that sweet. Monique kissed him before he left. He gave her three twenty to put up. He had told her to keep the door locked and if anyone knocked just be quiet and don't answer it. But –

The ride back to the Knights Inn was a blank trip.

Ted hit the steering wheel. "Damn it! I told'cha. Didn't I tell ya? Told'cha."

"Where he went at?"

"I don't know. Crack'h crazy, told'cha"!

They waited on the girl, who had been waiting on the sidewalk.

Ted asked her, "Where he went at.?"

"I don't know." She went to Pharaoh's side. "Something wrong wit' that man, let me in."

Pharaoh opened the door to a whiff of her body odor.

Then Ted asked her, "What he did?"

"He just shot out the room and took off in that damn truck."

Now with his nose in the window the short time it took for them to get back to Village Green, Pharaoh was glad to get out from the awkward scent of musky coochie and cheap perfume. The trick got out of the back seat and into the front, and he walked over and gave Ted two dime pieces, scouting the parking lot for the red Malibu. It was nowhere in sight.

Ted pointed at him. "Boy, you da man, shoulda been found ya." There were boys loitering around the mailboxes.

"Anytime ya catch uh lick like dis, just call me."

"Coulda made a lot more if you woulda listened to me," Ted hit his cigarette, "Told'cha he was crazy," He put those pieces in the ashtray along with the other six that he'd cuffed on the white man, "Coulda still been in the room."

"Baby," said the trick, "'Gon give me uh piece?"

Ted suddenly jerked his head her way. "Shut up, dat's my boy, and you don't ask him for shit." He then pulled off.

The squeaking sounds of breaks filled the night with the tweeting highs of six by nines – the dented up black Buick Regal turning in with that one bright and other dim headlight it had. Draco was driving, bouncing and smoking a blunt.

Pharaoh hollered him down.

And the breaks cried as Draco turned the music down, looking at him. "What up boy?"

"Can't call it," Pharaoh stepped to the window, smelling the fumes. Two boxes of Swisher's were on the seat. He pointed at them, "I'mma need two for the one I'mma copt."

"Alright, alright," Draco told him, "I got'cha. Jus re'd up on dat fire too." He reached under the seat and grabbed a brown paper bag, reached in the glove compartment and grabbed some baggies. "Boy, thought I was gonna have to help you wit' dat nigga at first."

Pharaoh hissed, "I ain't soft."

"Nigga ain't from here." Draco began stuffing the sack.

Pharaoh started to comment but changed his mind. He wasn't feeling any of what Richie and Draco were on. But just that statement alone had him wondering who in the hell Draco thought that he was. He paid him and walked off, bursting a blunt in the process. He would let Monique know he was back and was hustling awhile out there tonight.

CHAPTER 10

"Stop it Paul!" Rose jerked away and started veering towards the curve. "Leave me alone Paul!" She picked up an empty beer bottle and threw it at him. It burst in the middle of the road.

"Gone Paul"!

"You act like you don't know who I am."

"Paul!"

The yard of the crack-house was dark. Rose had been coming out for some fresh air when she'd bumped into Paul Russell. Now she wasn't about to get raped just because he thought he still had it like that.

"…Bring yo' motherfuckin' ass here!"

"Paul, if you keep walkin' up here, I'mma cut'cha ass!" She ran out in the road and picked up a piece of the broken bottle,

"Gone now!"

"You bedda not cut me wit' that goddamn bottle."

Paul approached and Rose swiped. He caught her arm and spun her around to him. The broken bottle fell out of her hand.

"Gone Paul!" she yelled.

"You act like you don't love me no mo'."

"Leave me alone Paul!"

One of the dope boys from 5ᵗʰ stepped out the trap, saw what was going down and said, "Hey nigga! Leave auntie 'lone," Rose wasn't his auntie but that's what he called her, "She don't fuck wit' nobody, and if she don't wanna be bothered, don't fuck wit' her and let her do her thang, or see me."

With that said, Rose jerked away and almost fell. She then started up the dark street, looking back to see if he was following her. He wasn't though. Now she wished that Deborah hadn't taken that boy nowhere, and, all that stuff Paul had done to her, slapping her around like a dog, pimping her, hitting her in the head with bottles, he was the devil. One day she had gotten tired and had picked up that butcher knife. If he had lifted that dirty white shirt of his up, she knew that ugly scar would still be there.

Cutting through some bushes, she came out on another road, heart still pounding. And a beige Monte Carlo was coasting up the side street. *Raw'd-Up!* She started running that direction, waving and hollering, "Raw'd-Up, Raw'd-Up!"

The beige Monte Carlo stopped.

And Rose flew up there to the window, scaring the shit out of him. "Raw'd-Up," she said, "I need you to take me home."

"What da hell wrong wit' you"?

"Nothing, I just wanna go home."

His dreadlocks swung from left to right and there was a sudden twist of his body. He looked out the back window, nostrils flared, wide eyed; peeping the scenery. He was a tall thirty-four year old with keen features and a few gold teeth. And he knew Rose because some serious dope charges had had him at Ester's office some years back. It had shocked him when he had gotten out of prison and had found out that Rose had started smoking. He was from 8th Avenue, and called his home the thuggish Gardenia projects, and during his incarceration he had touched basis with some real spiritual brothers. He hit the gas. "I gotta go OutEast first."

"I don't care."

He brushed his nose with a finger, his look puzzled. "You sure ain't nobody botherin' you, want Raw'd Up to do somethin' 'bout it?"

Rose looked off and cracked a smile, blocking out the bad memories of Paul.

They went OutEast – straight to the side of the rugged Lake Road projects that sat off of East University. Lake Road Slim was in the front circle drinking Heineken – tall, dark, a knife scar on his left forearm. He was about an inch taller than Raw'd-Up, whose dreads made him look around six-three. They were old friends, had both been to prison. The only difference now was that Raw'd-Up had changed a great deal but Lake Road Slim was still the same.

"Rose, what dey do,"

"Nothing… Raw'd-Up finna take me home. You seen ya auntie?"

"I thought she was with you, shit. Ya'll kept me up the other night,"

Lake Road Slim took the money from Raw'd Up. Then he left to get the ounce of dro.

And Rose lit a cigarette.

"You know I don't let nobody smoke in my car."

"Well, my bad." She was about to get out.

"It's a'ight since it's you."

"Boy, stop playing with me."

Rawd-Up laughed.

"You haven't been back to Ester lately, have ya?"

"I don't mess around no mo' to even put myself in that position."

"Bedda not, cause she worked uh miracle with that one."

"I wouldn't exactly call it uh miracle." Raw'd-Up grabbed the sack out of the ashtray. He took a few bumps and passed it to Rose. By now, Lake Road Slim was coming back.

"Uh…shit…" Rose said, "Uh year and a day for them charges you had, boy please." She took some bumps as the two talked. Last time she had some was when she had bumped into the both of them at Fletcher's. Then, before they left, she told Lake Road Slim that if he saw Deborah to let her know that she went home.

And he assured that he would.

They were pulling out when Raw'd-Up told her, "Twenty G's got that off of me, even had to sale my Cutlass to get that money up, 'cause Raw'd couldn't see no dime wit' dat lil' man hangin' off of'im."

The blinking traffic light of NE 31st Avenue and 15th Street, animated the darks essence with a flickering red and yellow glow. It was humid at 2am.

And Pharaoh had just walked to the corner smoking a blunt. He was lost in thought as he took the path back into the projects. He didn't notice that the boys up there were missing. As he crossed the parking lot headlights loomed up from out of nowhere. When he saw it sailing his direction, he dropped the blunt and kept straight ahead.

"Hey you, where you going"!

Blue and red flashes swarmed the entire area and two white officers jumped out.

"Hey! Stop right there!"

Pharaoh continued between two cars and threw his pill bottle under one of them. The short stout one came behind him. The tall spiteful one hurried to cut him off. He knew he was being harassed and got angry at the thought. He was just stepping on the sidewalk when they caught up with him.

"What're you doing out this late?"

"Walkin'," he told the tall one, who had a country accent and appeared to be a redneck in uniform, "Why ya'll messin' wit' me? I ain't did shit."

"Selling dope, aren't you?"

Pharaoh hissed and said, "Hell naw…"

The tall spiteful one had a nasty vibe in his crooked posture, leaning in Pharaoh's face a little. "Where're you coming from?"

"Minding my business," Pharaoh told him, "Where ya'll comin' from, redneck city? I ain't did shit for ya'll to be fuckin' wit' me."

"Oh – got ourselves a little slick one hey," The tall one grimaced, leaning back a tad bit.

Pharaoh knew they were about to search him and took them by surprise. He started talking shit as he suddenly made his way towards the police car. "I ain't got shit on me, ain't no dope," he was saying, "What? Uh lighter and thirty dollars in my pocket, uh cell-phone." After he told them his name and date of birth, he said, "Now I don't know my social security number or nothin' like that, but, I'm pur-ty sure, wit' da technology ya'll got nowadays, ya'll can figure it out." He sat his hands on the hood. "C'mon, let's gon' and get this shit over wit' so I can take my ass home and go to sleep, cause that's jus' where I was going."

The tall one's action was quick and unhesitant. It startled the young deputy, who seemed astonished by the sudden movement. "Alright smart-aleck," he fumed aggressively, slamming his fist down on the hood, "Funny guy."

Pharaoh gazed into the depths of those pulsing blue pupils. The stare didn't frighten him. Neither did the man's wrinkled face that grew redder by the second, which made the man's bushy blonde hair and decayed look, fit the criteria of a racist.

"Pat his ass down," The tall one snarled and walked off, "Must've hid it behind the dumpster."

Pharaoh shook his head as the young one began searching him. "Jus' don't plant no crack on me, ya'll good for dat shit. Hope it ain't no lil' baggies on the ground, cause ya'll uh love to hit uh nigga wit' uh ole paraphernalia charge."

"You need to shut up."

Pharaoh started laughing, until he saw what the tall one was picking up. By now, another squad car was coming up. "Dat shit ain't mine."

"Cuff him."

Man... *Look at dis flaw ass shit.* "Ain't mine," he snapped. But as soon as he saw how the tall one was coming, he put his hands behind his back. "No... want get dat lucky. I know ya nasty ass uh love to get da chance," *Crooked bitches!* "Ya'll betta be glad my back hurting, cause I woulda made ya'll run it tonight," *Nasty motherfucka's!*

Monique came out there when they were putting him in the car. She started screaming. All she had been planning to do was to tell him how late it was.

"Calm down ma'am."

"He ain't did nothin'."

It was the tall one that approached her when Pharaoh was hollering about bonding out. All the while, he was trying to get her eyes to follow his to the tail end of that Pontiac. It didn't take long, and he realized she was quick on catching on too. So he nodded in the backseat and yelled, "Dey ain't got shit on me. Bond me out!"

…And so the police car soon left with the tall one driving and making smart remarks. Pharaoh was driven by deep feelings at the sight of Monique, who was making her move as they disappeared out of view. It bothered him though. He couldn't shake the thought that he was somehow letting her down. After all, she was depending on his protection, wasn't she, that made him realize that she was his heart. He knew he wouldn't forgive himself if something ever happened to her. That was all he could think about the short ride down 39th Avenue, to the Alachua County Jail.

The procedures of booking didn't take too long. And a free call was like who to call. Then two guards stepped around the wall. One of them started putting down on him. Now he hadn't known that the tall one was still there until he saw him leaving with a snooty grin. What part of the game was telling the guards that he was trying to call the girl he had just beaten up? He wasn't booked under no damn battery. He told them that but they wouldn't listen. He should've known the tall one had been up to something when he had heard Monique scream, "Hell no!" But —

The two guards were forceful in making him step into a holding cell.

So he walked in with a straight look, hating the echo when the door slammed. *Shit is funky in here! Smell like feet, ass, and armpits!* He eyed the old black bum, who was lying down on the bench.

"That's him smellin' like that dawg," a red dude with cornrows stated, "Rank, ain't he?"

"Hell yeah," Pharaoh took a seat on the cold bench, frowning at the floor and the stench of piss by the silver toilet.

"What dey got'cha for dawg?"

"Uh half uh blunt and these motherfucka's act like ya gotta whole damn brick," Pharaoh snapped, then went into detail about how the tall one had played the game so dirty.

The red dude hissed, "Fuck motherfucka's got me for trespassing in Tree Trail, and I'm out there to my sista 'partment, tryin' to stop these ho's from fightin'."

Pharaoh shook his head.

And then the red dude stated, "Man, Gainesville gettin' creeper than uh bitch, swear I'm finna move away from this shit. Neva heard of uh nigga gettin' locked up on a sworn complaint. They got my cousin back there on 1H for that, heard he in the box now though."

A key entered the door.

And Pharaoh was called out last to see court services. After that, pass the nurse he'd already seen and on to be escorted to another holding cell. Then bangs struck a cell door. He bounced back, alarmed by the matter.

"I'm gon' kill you nigga! I'mma fuck you up boy!"

The black guard approached the cell. "Get off that damn door!"

"I'm tellin' you, you lucky they pulled me tonight fuck boy! 'Cause I was coming!"

Again, the black guard yelled. "Get off that damn door!"

Shocked to see Melvin raging like an ape, Pharaoh was forced to gaze at him. Then, seconds later, he fell into his uproar. "You ain't gon' do shit!" he yelled, "Come back to Village Green and I'mma –."

"Hey! Hey! Hey!" The black guard got control of the matter with the help of a sergeant.

After Pharaoh was pushed in a holding cell one door over, he could still hear Melvin's threats. But after he heard the guard's threats of spray, everything fell silent.

CHAPTER 11

"Cuz! Dis glass!" Richie said, "Where da hell you got dis shit from?"

Draco told him.

And Richie started rubbing his chin. "And you 'on't know da nigga's?"

Draco licked the blunt and said, "Naw…"

"Wondah if dey got some mo' of dis cuz."

Draco lit the blunt and said, "Probably. The way dat shit was set up was like the movies."

"What'cha mean cuz?"

Draco went to explaining.

And all the while his cousin talked Richie was thinking.

Monique balled up at 5am when her cramps kicked in. Lying on Pharaoh's mattress, she was worried to death. Was he coming home? Were they going to keep him in jail? What was he charged with anyway? She wanted to go downstairs and call. His money was in his top drawer where she had put it at and she could find out about bonding him out. But it was just that slim possibility of Melvin catching her in there. And oh my

God! What would happen then? She truly feared Melvin now – feared what he would do to her after what had happened. Pharaoh was all she had. The only person she'd been able to turn to. And she loved him for it.

Eyes red, she got up and took care of her issue, staring in the mirror at her face. Sakena was asleep on the mattress too.

What if Melvin suddenly busted in there? She cried and cried. By eight he still wasn't there. And a knock scared her shitless. It couldn't be him. He would've said her name. Matter of fact, didn't he have his key? And it couldn't be his momma. He had told her that his mother knocked real hard, then who, Melvin? Had somebody ratted her being up there. But the knock stopped and she relaxed a bit. Still, when Sakena awoke she was crying.

Pharaoh was R.O.R the next morning, probably blessed that first appearance had had one of the most lenient judges in the city that some of the boys had nicknamed 'Turn'em loose'. The long walk from jail, across Waldo Road, and up 31st Avenue, was tiresome with the sunrays beaming majestically.

Richie and Draco were coming up the sidewalk.

"Damn Pharaoh!" Richie said, "Where da hell you been? We been lookin' for ya lil' boney ass all morning."

"Jail," He approached them with a curious look, wondering why they had been looking for him, "Why? What's up?"

"Oh," Draco said, "Dat was you dey was fuckin' wit' last night."

"We need your help wit'uh lick," Richie cut in.

A *lick!* He felt extremely uncomfortable, and when Richie tapped Draco, he saw Richie smirking. "Man… what is ya'll talkin' about."

"It's uh sweet lick," Draco said, "Uh dope house. I copt uh cookie from this nigga last night. Dey strong, it's gonna be easy too boy." He nodded his head at Pharaoh, who appeared to look militant.

"Me and cuz been plottin' dis since last night," Richie came with, "We just need one mo' person cause cuz can't go in there. Even if he did have uh mask on, nigga's still might peep who he is, and I can't go in there 'olo." Richie seemed strained in his demeanor. "Now, I know we done had our lil' problems in da past," he continued, stretching out his fat arms, "But look my nigga, we from the projects, all of us," He dropped his arms. "It's like we done settled our differences and shit cause we older. And I know ya real, dats why I told cuz we gon' step to ya." He tapped Draco. "Didn't I cuz?"

"You said it."

"Me and you run up in dat bitch Pharaoh," Richie didn't hesitate to say, "Dope, money, weed, whatever –," He punched the palm of his fat hand, "Guaranteed from what cuz told me. And I know somebody who'll let me hold two AK's."

"Hold on, hold…" Pharaoh eyed them suspiciously, seeing their serious look. "Man, how ya'll know dat shit gon' be easy?"

"When I went in da house," Draco came with, "Gave da nigga the money and he told me to stay by the door. Nigga jus' went in da kitchen and grabbed one of dem thangs out da cabinet boy. I can give ya da scoop on the inside too." He stepped back. "See, it's uh room –."

"Hold on, hold on, hold…" Pharaoh eyed them. "Man…."

"For real," Richie said, "No bullshit, so ya know I ain't lying."

Pharaoh thought a second. "I tell ya what? Gimme uh minute and I'll be back there to holler at'chall."

"A'eight," Richie said, "We'll be to da crib."

Now by the time Pharaoh got upstairs he already had a bad vibe about it. But he opened the door and got punched in the stomach, and the whole matter changed then.

"Damn…." He slumped to the floor, his head just above her pretty little feet. She had knocked the wind out of him. "Why da hell you punched me?" He crazily looked up at her.

"For going to jail and leaving me," Monique told him, with glossy red eyes. Then she punched him in the side.

"Damn girl! Dat shit hurt! You know I'm boney!" He popped up, looking at her.

Monique was already looking in his eyes. "It 'pose to hurt," she told him, and then hugged him. "Don't do that no more. I was really worried Pharaoh."

Sakena pranced up, "Hey Pairoh."

"What up pretty girl?"

Sakena chuckled, "Momma wa cry'n Pairoh."

"You wasn't cryin' was you?"

"Nope, me big girl"!

Wiping her face, Monique muttered, "And I got your stuff last night too." Her voice was sketchy, and, trying to look mad, she knew her feelings were opposite.

Pharaoh met her stare. "Ya know, you look real… sexy when ya mad." He went in his room and took off his shirt. "C'mon, I know what'cha need."

"You think you do don'tcha," She stood in the doorway with an interesting stare, squinting her eyes at him and bouncing that right leg of hers, "You can't get it right now… all the stress you put me through knocked my monthly on." Mad because she couldn't, she went in his top drawer and threw him his pill bottle.

"Ah… ya baby-daddy in jail"!

"Stop lying!" Delirious, she saw his straight look. "What he did?"

"I don't know."

CHAPTER 12

Later that afternoon Monique was downstairs. Melvin had some serious charges – DUI, resisting arrest with violence, and two counts of battery on a Leo. The news at twelve had made it very clear. They had even showed Melvin's mug shot. It had taken five officers to bring him down and he had broken one officer's jaw. The other officer had a wrist injury. She couldn't believe it.

Still, the phone was ringing off the hook. And twelve out of the seventeen messages she had erased had all been recordings from the county jail. The first five had been threats – two from Tina, three devastating one's from Melvin. But the last of the five had really spooked her, being left at eleven fifty-nine last night. Melvin had sworn that he was on his way to cut her throat and kill Pharaoh. By the way he was talking she could tell that he had been on heavy alcohol. She had hung up and thought. That had been around the time Pharaoh had come back and had left with that man again.

A knock came. She moved the curtains back to see a woman with his friend from the other day. Somebody must've told him that Pharaoh was down there. Well, she couldn't tell him where Pharaoh had run off too, but a phone call would. Or would it?

…In Richie and Draco's apartment, Pharaoh answered the cell in a voice so criminal that he didn't even notice. They were all sitting around a small round kitchen table. Richie was the only one sitting on a stool which was strong enough to hold his weight. After telling Monique he'll be up there in a minute, he hung up and leaned back in the chair.

"So, I'mma get the AK's," Richie said, "Dat's all we gon' need."

"Hold on …I'mma need somethin' too now," Draco suggested.

"Damn cuz!" Richie wailed, "All you gotta do is drive, but I'mma get'cha somethin' anyway." He then told him to go get that and show him.

And Draco left.

Then, Richie gazed across the table at him, "So, what'cha think?"

"I think we gon' have to come in there bussin' so nigga's know we ain't 'bout dat bullshit," Pharaoh told him, "Just cause Draco say dat shit gon' be easy don't mean that it's going down dat way. And I hope you ain't scared to shoot uh motherfucka wit' me doin' all da damn running."

"Nigga, I got'cha"! Richie popped the collar of his huge blue coogie shirt. "Now, if you want me to do it, I'll do it. Ain't shit scared 'bout me and you know it."

Pharaoh thought on that a second. He knew Richie really didn't want that job and could tell by that look. Besides, Richie was too fat and slow, and he knew Richie knew that. But having the biggest job made him ponder rather or not they were using him for their own means to come up. Then again, the concept of more dope and money outweighed the fact that he didn't trust them. So just before Draco came back and handed Richie the cookie, he said, "Nigga, I got it."

"Glass," Richie dropped it on the table, where it made a keen, solid sound on the brown wood, "China white," he roared.

"Damn," Pharaoh picked it up – aware that not a single piece had broken off, "Is dis shit real?"

"Yeah," Richie said, "Not tryin' to start nothing, but your momma just sent the message back dat it's da best dope I ever sold her, sendin' people here cause she still owe me my damn twenty dollars." He paid close attention to how Pharaoh was studying it. Then he smirked and told Draco, "Put it back up cuz, we gotta run and go get these thangs."

Handing it back, Pharaoh said, "Lemme copt two befo' ya go."

And Draco said, "I'll giv' ya two, we in dis together."

Monique was sitting on the sofa having a very interesting conversation with Michelle. Michelle was very bright skinned with thin lips and talked very sophisticated. She didn't know why Pharaoh's friend would bring her there knowing how her face looked. She felt embarrassed, but she figured his friend had told her what had happened though.

"I've been studying for awhile now," Michelle was saying, "You can trace the roots from Africa to the lost city of Atlantis."

"You really believe there was a lost city called Atlantis?"

"Of course, perfect walls were found under there. Edgar Cayce talked about it. The sleeping prophet they called him. Why do you think the ocean is named the Atlantic Ocean?"

"I never knew."

"There were a lot of ancient civilizations. Atlantis was just one of them. A flood covered the land of Mesopotamia too. And the people of Atlantis were closely related to the Egyptians."

"The pyramids fascinate me."

"Energy, they were masters of science and the celestial realms."

"What do you mean?"

"The stars, planets, unseen worlds, the heavens, we're talking about high civilization here. These people were highly spiritually advanced. Aztecs, Mayans, Incas, Olmecs, and the list go on."

There was silence when the door opened. Pharaoh came in looking crazy. Michelle's blue Cherokee had been parked out there, and Boochie was wearing a Gucci outfit with a kangol on.

"What up dawg?"

"Not shit," Pharaoh answered strangely, still looking crazy, "What up wit' you?"

They stepped out and left the girls talking. Michelle was saying something about an ancient temple.

Now the boys' two doors down were in and out of their door. One had told Boochie that Pharaoh was down there. But Pharaoh hadn't known that Kitty was in her sister's apartment. He was just about to say something when she stepped out across the way, seeing him. She was in her usual – short shorts, halter top, her hair done and siddity.

"Oh, so dat's where da bitch stay at I heard you been out here fighting about," she said sarcastically, rolling her neck, "The one you almost got'cha back broke about, and fat Richie had to pull a gun on him just to get him off ya."

"Don't know what da fuck ya heard," he told her, "But you got da Pharaoh fucked up."

"Well, somebody needs to tell her she uh silly bitch for wanting uh nobody like you."

He shot her a bird.

Then Boochie turned his back to one of the boys' two doors down. "Man, what you chillin' down here for?"

Pharaoh started laughing. "Who told'cha I was down here?"

Boochie gestured towards the boys.

And so Pharaoh filled him in – his arrest, his encounter with Melvin in there and what they had said about him on the news. But he damn showl wasn't going to tell him what Richie and Draco had stepped to him with. He was still thinking about that one.

Boochie shook his head. "Boy –."

"Tell me about it dawg." He pulled a sack from his pocket. "Wanna smoke?"

"Naw… not right now," He rubbed his chin, "Really just stopped by to holler at'cha."

"Holler at me how?"

Boochie looked at him. "Was close by, jus' came by to see what you was doing."

"Hot as it is dawg, not shit."

They talked for awhile. Eventually, after ten minutes, Michelle came to the door and told Boochie about the time. And it wasn't long before they left.

Pharaoh decided to fix himself a bowl of Captain Crunch.

Monique came in there. "Michelle is –."

"I don't wanna hear nothin' about her… she got my dawg head all fucked up."

"What, you're not happy for them?"

"It's not that." He ate a scoop.

"Well, I understand. I'll feel kinda bad too."

"Feel bad 'bout what?" He lowered his brows.

Monique studied him. "What, he didn't tell you."

"Tell me what?"

"About Orlando," she stated weirdly, "They're moving in a couple days."

Pharaoh frowned. "He ain't tell me no shit like dat,"

"Well, that's what she said. And he didn't deny it because he was standing right there when she told me."

"Oh yeah"!

Monique nodded.

He soon took a shower and hopped in the bed. She left Sakena watching cartoons in the living room and lied down with him.

"My dawg ain't tell me 'cause he ain't going, he aint stupid."

"Well, I'm finna get it off ya mind." She slid his boxers down and was soon pleasing him with her mouth.

Pharaoh wasn't worried about it. He was having second thoughts about the lick. Or if Richie and Draco were planning to use him he knew he wasn't playing the fool.

CHAPTER 13

The smell of gas fumes casted a deadly feeling as the dented up black Buick Regal crept through unfamiliar territory. Shadows in the night marked the few addicts that drifted the errie roads, wandering like zombies.

"You need to fix dat gas leak cuz."

"Bad ain't it?"

"Got me feelin' sick cuz"!

Pharaoh was nauseated in the back seat and anxious to get it over with. The AK sat in his lap. A blue backpack was on his back. A black ski mask sat on the tip of his head, ready to be snatched down. He had been inspired when Richie had showed him their accessories. They'd come and got him an hour ago. He had left Monique cooking. Had told her that he'll be back in a minute, knowing dirt was up his sleeve.

The car crept along for what it seemed like miles. Then the headlights faded – a near street light bringing about a wicked impression upon the strange hood, like an alien presence. The breaks cried and pierced the silence as they slowly neared the curve. And then it stopped.

"The house on da right, ya'll make it quick."

"Cuz, keep it in drive."

"Hey, man…" Pharoah peered at the house across the road then stared at Draco in disbelief. "It's bedda if ya park in da yard, ain't like uh fence up or you pullin' on da grass or somethin', it's uh clear escape, we won't draw attention like we are now, cause right here we look like jack boys, don'tcha think dat's bedda?" A strange awareness took over him and he began to question their capabilities. Deep down inside he felt that they didn't have a clue about robbing.

"He right cuz. All we have to do is jump off da porch and in da car."

"Alright, alright," Draco moved the sawed-off 12 gauge pump, pressed the gas and hit the lights.

"No! Bend da block nigga. You think nigga's don't see us now. It won't look right if we just pull up and park now. Gotta ride 'round and give it 'bout fifteen minutes, then bend back and pull up in da yard like we comin' to copt. It ain't time to be slippin'," Pharaoh was saying as they turned to go straight ahead, "Gotta be up on heavy game now, we finna rob!" He frowned in disgust. As they rode by, he could see a glow through the window of the crack-house.

They took a brief ride and discussed it again. By the time they pulled in the yard, they were ready. Both doors flew open at the cry of the breaks. Before the car stopped, Pharaoh was already out on Draco's side, but Richie was just making it out on his. It was now or never. After Richie dashed up the steps in a clumsy run of a fat boy, Pharaoh was right behind him hearing the burst when the door blasted open.

Richie stumbled in with the AK raised and hollered, "Get da fuck down!"

Loud yells and commotion seem to spring up from everywhere. But gunshots minimized movements and two crack-heads hit the floor. A ripple of bullets sprayed up the counter that two dope boys ducked behind. Glass jars shattered! The kitchen window burst! Bullets ate up the wooden walls!

Richie blanked out of it and scurried to a closed room door, where he launched into it shoulder first, leaving it cock-sided on the bottom hinge. "Get da fuck out!" he told a chubby boy and a dark chick, who were already on the floor from the gunshots still being heard.

Pharaoh had come in shooting and was still doing it until he rushed around the counter, gun on both of them. One had an arm full of tattoos. "Do what da fuck I tell ya and you won't get bust."

In a matter of seconds, six people were face down in the living room. Richie stood by the door with the AK on them while Pharaoh went through the cabinets.

Ain't shit in here! He nervously glanced back at Richie to make sure everything was under control, fully aware of the pots he'd shot, glass, and steaming water all over the floor. He went under the sink, heart racing, saw nothing and yanked the refrigerator door. *Oh shit!* He looked at Richie then sat the AK on the shot up counter, a bit excited at finding three cookies of crack cocaine. Paranoid, he wrapped the plastic around them and put them in the backpack. He grabbed the AK, glanced at Richie, and rushed to the room.

"Empty ya'll pocket's!" Richie demanded, "Everything!" Greed was in his eyes. When the chubby boy didn't move, he kicked him, "A'eight, play wit' it."

Now the girl was the second one that kicked out. And Richie was blowed by the amount of money she had on her. He blinked with a stern look at the rings on her fingers. She had long, silky black hair. And he made her roll over just to get a good look at her. Three gold chains were around her neck. And she was fine as a motherfucka too.

Inside the room, Pharaoh was loading his pockets. He had flipped the mattress off of the bed and had found money, a loaded .45, and small blocks of rocked up cocaine. Nervous and thinking crazy, he decided that he couldn't make his pockets bulge. After he packed some in his socks, he put everything else in the backpack. He then looked under the bed and went to the closet, nothing. He rambled through the dresser drawers – nothing but a crack pipe and tiny pebbles of crack. He then picked up the AK and peeped around the corner before he came out, noticing Richie bent over stuffing money in his socks. He realized that Richie didn't notice him until he stepped over the girl.

"A'eight," Richie said, "Move if ya wanna, I'll murda all of ya'll." He back peddled out and onto the porch, where he turned around and clumsily stumbled down the steps, then sloppily plunged into the front seat.

Draco stumped the gas. "Did'chall get it?"

"Drive!" Pharaoh yelled, wondering why Draco hadn't shot at those figures approaching. Then the headlights popped on the second he saw them jumping out of the way. Gunshots filled the night! They turned the corner, wheels squealing. The ass end skidded sideways. The left back wheel hit the grass before it caught grip on the road and they shot off.

The smell of gas fumes arose stronger than before as the Regal reached greater speeds, racing down the street.

"Did ya'll get it? I know ya'll got it?"

"We got it cuz," Richie said, smirking as he took the mask off. "Yeah," He slung his fat arm across the seat for some dap,

"Yeah nigga!"

Pharaoh gave him some dap. He was excited too. "Draco, slow dis bitch down man… You don't wanna get pulled and dat's how ya drivin', like ya wanna get pulled. Calm down nigga." He grinned as the car slowed, "Get in some traffic and take dis bitch back to da green nigga. Don't hit no… back roads."

Back at Richie and Draco's apartment a half hour later, the small round table held five grand, three ounces of crack, seven ounces of cocaine, and a fully loaded .45. Stunned by the discovery of what had been in the backpack had the two cousins quarrelling. And Pharaoh was shocked by their actions.

"I'm gettin' da two ounces. You can't sell crack like I can. You fuck up too much money cuz!"

"No, you do, all the time and wanna blame shit on me. You fucked up da last one." Draco rushed the table but his cousin stepped in front of him.

"Cuz, you ain't touchin' da crack! You act stupid wit' it!"

"Get da fuck out my way!" Draco pushed him in the stomach but his cousin didn't budge.

"A'eight. I'mma hit'cha and knock ya ass out now." Richie backed up and flinched at him.

"Hit me ya want too."

Mesmerized by their actions, Pharaoh stepped to the table. "Well, I'm gettin' seventeen hundred. Dat leave ya'll wit' sixteen fifty uh piece. We gotta ounce of crack uh piece, well, I don't know how ya'll gon' do ya'lls, and I'm gettin' two ounces of soft, so dat's fair." *Cause ya'll nigga's actin' stupid!* He couldn't believe it.

Richie began thinking over the matter, until it hit him, "Okay." Everything was quiet as Pharaoh counted the money. Richie and Draco never took their eyes off of him.

"I don't want the pistol," *Get da hell away from ya'll silly nigga's!* He figured if he took his shirt off they would notice.

Richie said, "I'm gettin' da pistol. So it ain't even no reason in thinkin' 'bout it cuz."

"Damn, you already got pistols," Draco cried, watching Pharaoh carrying away his share, "I'm gettin' da pistol!" He rushed the table.

Richie pushed him. "No you ain't cuz!"

"I'm gone!" Outside, Pharaoh took his shirt off and put his share in it. He could still hear them arguing as he hurried off.

Rose stepped out of her apartment back there and strolled out to the parking lot. Linda's car was back. But wasn't that her son cutting the corner up there. Didn't he have his shirt off? And hadn't he been holding something? She was pretty sure that it had been him.

She had only come back home to take a quick shower and send Deborah over to the Big One, still speeding over the good stuff he had. Yes, she had sent the message back that it was the best dope he had ever sold her, and now all her and Deborah seem to be doing was riding around and making money to come back and spend with him.

She turned around, streaking in those little footsteps she had. Now that Linda's car was back, she would go back to her apartment and tell Deborah to gone on over there. Then they could ride back to Crosstown and probably do the same thing all over again. But she would bet a dime piece to anybody's two dollars that it had been her son leaving from back there.

Monique stepped aside. "Where you been Pharaoh?" She closed the door and started bouncing that leg.

"Girl, you trippin'"!

"And what do you have in the shirt?"

"None of your business," he said teasingly, then went in the room.

"Oh, it's my business." She stopped in the doorway. "Where the hell you been Pharaoh, and why you ain't take ya cell phone?"

He sat on the bed, smiling at her hint of vulgarness, "You trippin'."

"No I'm not Pharaoh!" She stepped to him, standing over him, "Ya damn food cold, I'mma warm it up though, and I hope you ain't planning on going nowhere else tonight!"

"Damn…" he cried, "Is you like this every month?"

Monique paused a second, "Okay, I'm sorry. But I'm still being nosey." She reached for the shirt.

"Damn…" He unfolded it, grinning at his belongings, "Seventeen hundred, put it up somewhere."

Monique was stunned. She'd saw drugs before but never that much. However, when more of that and money came out of his pockets and socks, she said, "Oh my God, Pharaoh, who you done robbed?" When he told her to count it she nervously sat down. After she finished, her heart was racing. "This is two thousand, and you said that was seventeen hundred, so you got –." She cut off her sentence, gazing at him. "What you did?"

"Nothing"!

"Stop lying Pharaoh, go to jail again and I'mma kick ya ass, who you robbed?"

"No…" He shook his head, "I neva tell my dirt. Ain't gon' tell on my damn self dat's fo' showl. If I go to jail, I just fucked up. I'm tired of being po'," he told her, "So let it go Monique. Just let it go." He laid back. "Just chill, and ball wit' da Pharaoh". *Uh po' nigga got money now.*

Richie was locked in his auntie's cluttered up room with all the dope and the pistol. He began counting all the money the girl had had on her – mostly hundreds, quite a few fifty's, a twenty every so often. He was approaching forty one hundred when Draco began beating on the door.

"Cuz!" he hollered, "I'm tellin' ya, keep beatin' on that goddamn door and I know somethin'!"

"Fuck you!" Draco shouted, "You always tryin' me!"

Richie browsed over everything on the bed. "Ain't my fault you don't know how to sell dope."

"Nigga, some of dat shit in there mine"!

Richie didn't say anything.

"And dat lady still out here waitin' on yo ass,"

Richie paused on forty nine hundred, saying, "What lady?"

A long pause from Draco behind the door, then he thundered:

"The lady dat be wit' Rose!"

"And what she got?"

"Forty dollars nigga, now gimme my shit"!

Richie tossed a blanket over the dope and told him, "You just need to stick to weed cuz."

"Well, you gon' gimme some money for it or somethin' nigga, think I'm just finna be alright wit' dis money we done split. Always think you just gon' try me. You ain't finna try me like dat!"

Richie thought a second and counted out three hundred. He opened the door and gave him that along with what to give Rose's smoking partner. He then told him, "Now leave me da fuck alone cuz!" And then he slammed the door and locked it.

CHAPTER 14

Over the next few days, Pharaoh laid low. He had found a cantaloupe colored '84 Caprice Classic that he'd bought for sixteen hundred. It was in Monique's name though. He didn't have any license. A trip to the Oaks Mall had Monique wearing sexy lingerie. Now that her period was off, she felt so sexy wearing it for him. He had bought Sakena a big Barbie castle and more dolls.

It was that Thursday morning that seemed all like a dark illusion. As Pharaoh lay in bed, he could hear Monique on the phone going off on Tina. Sakena had woke him up with her little taps talking about, "Mommy tay tum eat Pairoh." He just lied there, thinking. In the dream he'd had Richie had caught him stuffing the dope. His mind was starting to mess with him.

In the living room came the tunes of Scooby-Doo. Sakena sat on a towel and was eating her breakfast, watching it.

Monique finally hung up the phone and gave him his plate. She was hot. If Tina did think she was coming to get Sakena, then Tina certainly had another thing coming. Melvin hadn't got shot at, maybe jumped, and the mentioning of Pharaoh's name frightened her but, she wasn't no slut, two cent whore, or the biblical image Jezebel. Such cruel words for a suppose to be Christian who went to church every Sunday, and, if she was going to hell for what had happened, then she would probably see Tina down there burning too. She was pissed. How could Tina mention taking

71

her in because her drunk behind daddy hadn't done nothing but beat on her? How, when Tina had sat around the house and watched her son do the same damn thing? Of course, that wiry voice was still in Monique's ear, and she knew if Tina was there now she would rip that ugly mole right off the side of her fat face. That was the part she told Pharaoh and he started laughing.

"Alright, don't let dat woman come over here and beat you up now."

"Real funny Pharaoh"!

"You hate her that much?"

"I can't stand her. She's uh fake – Christian."

 "You sure about that,"

Monique gave him the eye, and started to grab that biscuit out of his plate and shove it in his mouth. But then she thought to tell him, "Oh, and ya momma came by looking for you. I told her you were sleep."

"What momma wanted?"

"She said she needed twenty dollars real bad, so I gave it to her. Was that alright with you?"

He nodded. After all, it was just momma like usual. And his pockets were looking pretty damn good.

"I offered to do her hair. She says she's gonna let me do it one day."

Pharaoh was hearing her but he really wasn't hearing her. Something strange was going on inside of him. But he would walk back there to see what was up with Richie and Draco.

…Now it was nothing out of the ordinary for what was going on, that was, when Pharaoh got back there an hour later to kind of like feel things out. Richie was talking shit to some boy that owed him and Draco some money. And from what Pharaoh could understand, the boy's brother owed both of them too. It seemed that Richie wasn't sweating it too much at first. Until –

Draco stepped out the door in shorts, no shirt, and tennis shoes, "Ya'll nigga's always 'bout dat pussy shit."

Richie started smirking, "Cuz, what'cha finna do?" The red boy started backing up.

And Richie hollered, "On't ah… Don't run now."

Draco caught him out in the parking lot and started dragging him out of the car. A tall, dark boy hopped out. Richie caught him in the chest and knocked him down damn near two cracks in the sidewalk away.

"Out here hidin' in da car," Richie yelled, "Ya'll nigga's bedda get dat money up!"

There was no spark of action in the tall one when he got up. Richie jacked him up and started talking shit to him. All the while this took place Draco was in the road getting it down with the other one. From how close Pharaoh stood, it seemed to be a pretty close throwing of hands to him. The boy was boxing good. Until –

Draco scooped him up and plowed up the asphalt with him. It was a done deal.

"Ya'll must think big Richie done fell soft 'round here. Me and cuz just been sparin' ya'll nigga's."

"Tired of all ya'll nigga's tryin' me!"

Richie looked at him. "What, ya talkin' to me or somethin' cuz?" Draco kept walking pass him.

Pharaoh didn't know what was going on but followed and told Draco what he needed.

And Richie hung by the open door while Pharaoh waited, pushing his shades back on his face.

"What's goin' on toothpick?"

"Can't call it,"

Richie glanced around, smirking, "Nigga's 'bout dat bullshit. Playing wit' money dis early in da mornin'," He seemed to browse over him before he decided to tell him, "…And ya momma tried to ease home dis mornin' after she got dropped off."

Pharaoh didn't comment. Now he knew what his mother had needed them twenty dollar's for. But if Richie ever dreamed of laying a hand on her, it was going to be war like he'd never brought it.

Draco came out and sold him the sacks.

Then, smirking at his cousin, Richie looked at Pharaoh, "But tell da truth though, me and cuz put'cha up on uh nice one, didn't we?"

"I told'chall it was gon' be easy."

"Yeah, cuz was right, but tell da truth though, we put'cha up on a decent one, ain't it?"

Hissing under his breath, Pharaoh said, "It was alright."

"I finna lock dis bitch down."

And so a grin struck Pharaoh's face. He told them he'll holler and left. Then again, if Richie actually felt like they'd put him on, did Draco think the same way, but the hell with that. The truth was more than evident now. He'd cuffed and Richie didn't know about it, while Richie had cuffed and thought that he hadn't seen him.

CHAPTER 15

The green Delta Eighty-Eight cruised through one side of the Lake Road Projects and was soon cruising through the other one.

In the circle, Lake Road Slim went inside and grabbed his pistol. It was about the fifth time he'd seen that car creeping through today.

Rose crossed 5th Avenue and hopped in Deborah's little red truck. All because the Big One hadn't been home the truth had come to light a short while ago. All the time it had been her son who had been selling Deborah them nice ass jugglers.

Fletcher's was thick and the traffic was slow and heavy, Deborah crunk up her truck in her eagerness to leave the parking lot. She was thinking about getting something from Slim. She said, "I hope he home."

Rose was chewing on her jaw and looking around. Most of the people she knew. She finally said, "Girl, I'm still wondering why you ain't been… said nothing."

"Well, Rose, I didn't know that was your son."

There was no such thing as coincidences to her. So a flash of reality hit Rose when she told Deborah to go left. How close she had been to finding out – the fight she'd heard about in which Deborah had driven her up there. She had come back and had told her that the girl's face was terrible, never mentioning his nickname but simply calling him my baby.

They finally caught a break in traffic. It had been a long three minute wait. And they passed that trick with all those dark spots in her face that Deborah didn't like too much. Rose, gazing ahead, now understood that her son had been the one Deborah had rented the truck too. So she kind of cracked her eyes at her friend, then she decided not to ask her, knowing how they both supported their habits.

"I wonda'h how that girl face look now"?

"Pretty good," Rose said, "Last time I saw her, you really couldn't see nothing."

"And I wonda'h if she the same girl that was out there with him that day?" Deborah lit a cigarette, mentioning, "She had uh nice hair-do, and I think a little girl was with her."

"Probably her," Rose yelped, "Cause she gotta lil' daughter."

"Well, his number still in the ashtray if you change your mind about calling him."

They slowed for the stop sign ahead. A man rode across on a bicycle. No! A bum! No! A smoker! Rose blinked. It was Paul Russell!

Pharaoh stepped back in that night and found Monique in the crimson nightgown. It was silk with thin straps and the length just at the bottom of her butt cheeks. He grabbed more dope and went back out. It was moving a little. Rumor had it that Richie and Draco had left in a rental car earlier.

The fiend in the red truck had spent with him two times already today. The last time she had been snickering. Whatever that was about, Pharaoh didn't know. He saw police and went back inside.

Monique's eyes followed his. "It look cute on me baby?"

"Of course"!

"Uh-huh," She smiled, "Ya probably just tellin' me that 'cause you ready again."

"You da one dat's ready."

They were soon going at it for the third time today. Sakena had fallen asleep on the living room floor next to her Barbie castle. It was one of those big ones with stairs, several rooms, and the kitchen, Monique's nails and feet were done. All she knew to do was to love Pharaoh. And pleasing him was the main thing. For the past days, they'd been having sex like crazy.

They were talking a half hour later when Pharaoh got Baser Ted's call. He wouldn't make the same mistake as he had the last time. He was soon in the kitchen cutting up most of what Richie had called china white. Monique popped up beside him and went to talking. She really didn't want him selling dope. It wasn't a secret though, they were both in love. This was his girl now. And though she had his manhood sore, nothing was going to happen to her, absolutely nothing.

CHAPTER 16

Waldo Road soon turned into Williston Road after crossing University Avenue; and the skimpy headlights of the soft ticking Datsun was small compared to the vast area that others filled. The store on the corner of SE 4th Street finally came into view minutes later. They didn't make that left by it but, rather breezed through the light and kept straight ahead, slowing to get ready to make that U, then quick right into the infamous Sugarhill projects. They waited for a break in traffic. The apartments were red brick and spaced like little houses, appearing ruthless in the night's essence. A chain link fence ran down beside it blocking it off from Williston Road. Dark images crossed the road ahead, dreadlock boys! For they knew those boys were coming out of that one way in, one way out road, well known as 'da bottom'.

Pharaoh didn't know that they had to pick up girls first. Neither did he know that they were going to Sands Motel until a sort of cute one with big breast got in and mentioned it. That motel was on SW 13th Street – prostitute stroll and police lane. People were known for getting roped off out there. What the hell was Baser Ted up too?

Raw'd-Up was putting gas in his car when a gray Lexus pulled to the opposite pump. The store on the corner of University Avenue and

Waldo Road always stayed busy. He hung up the nozzle and twisted his cap. Was cranking up when he seen her and recognized her. That was Patricia. Bobby Owens Patricia. He hadn't seen that fine black bitch in awhile. It spooked him a little bit. He grabbed his phone and called Lake Road Slim, pulling off while strangely looking at her. Off to the side were two boys standing by the pay phones. She seemed to be approaching them.

The past was the past, and Raw'd-Up knew that Patricia was nothing to be messed up with. She was poison. Her brother was murdered and he knew that she was the one responsible for having him killed. Her brother had snitched on him — the reason he'd caught his charges. However, that was awhile ago, and after all that, they say Patricia was down in Ft. Lauderdale. What was she doing back here now?

"Crack'h be spendin', don't he?" Ted was saying as he eased up beside Pharaoh. It was half past twelve, and the nerdy man had spent over three hundred already, "Crack'h got some money, don't he?"

Pharaoh nodded.

The tricks were naked in bed and the white man was stoned wearing white boxers. Running out of the beige dope a half hour ago had brought about the news of the china white, and the switch had almost caused an uproar in the man until Ted had been the first to take a hit. Now everything was silent except for the flickering sounds of lighters.

"That's some good dope ya got," Ted mumbled.

"Oh yeah"!

"Yeah man." Ted's mouth was still moving. It was if he was trying to say more but couldn't. Yet that didn't stop him from glancing back and making frugal gestures to the girls. Then he repeated, "Yeah man."

Another sell and another fifty, then the sort of cute one talked the white man into going into the bathroom with her. And the one from the time before got up and got dressed like excuse me but I got to go. But the white man reared out all too soon and caught her about to leave.

"Hey! What're you –?" The white man's stoned eyes were bulk.

"Hey! Give me my damn wallet!"

All hell broke loose in an instance, pandemonium like nothing else. A high pitched, shrieking squeal escaped from the trick as she snatched away to get out the door.

Ted sprung into action with a pocket knife, crotched low, jugging at him, yelling, "Back up crack'h!"

The sort of cute one scooped up her clothes and shot out of the room butt naked.

And Pharaoh was right behind her when she got in with her titties swinging like big balloons, looking straight stupid.

"Baby, where you got dat stuff from?" she asked, "Dat's dat naked?"

Pharaoh couldn't comment. He was stuck at the sight of Baser Ted coming out that room. The last thing he saw was the white man chasing them and heard a smack on the back window.

The trick was scurrying on down 13th Street now, and they picked her up, pushing it back to Sugarhill, where both tricks were dropped off. Some hundreds had been split. Pharaoh had ended up with two because they had wanted more.

And so by the time they were passing 23rd Avenue, Ted was yapping about everything, until they finally turned down 31st with a single police car trailing them. Then, seconds later, those colorful lights decorated the darkness.

Ted crushed his can of Schlitz Malt and jammed it under the seat. "Damn!"

"Man…" Pharaoh cried, "That man done told on you."

"Naw… man"!

"What da fuck you mean naw…" Pharaoh snapped, boney arms swinging. He was still a little hot, "You got license, don'tcha?"

It was then Ted said, "Got uh warrant."

"Uh warrant," Pharaoh cried, "Aw… man…"

"And it looks like that's dat nasty crack'h too," He hit the steering wheel, "He know my damn car!"

"Push dis bitch!" Pharaoh hollered, acting crazy. "I got dope nigga. I ain't goin' to jail tonight. Go!"

The Datsun sped up but soon slowed.

"What da fuck ya slowin' up for, go!"

Ted seemed confused in his high mental state, responding like, "Might be able to talk him out of it."

"What?" Outraged at him pulling over, Pharaoh began fumbling with the latch. Just before the car stopped he felt the need to hit him but knew he could get away. He shoved the door open and struck out, running wide open.

"Hey! Stop right there!"

There was a baffling look in Rose's eyes as she sped back to Deborah's truck. She had finally built up enough courage to ask her son. But he hadn't been there. In her hand was another twenty that she'd gotten from Monique. She had sworn she'd needed an excuse for stopping by. She looked at Deborah.

"Well, was he there?"

"Ont-ah girl"!

Deborah wanted to know what was up, "Well… what?"

Rose tapped her on the leg and yelped, "Girl… you shoulda seen what that child had on." She went into detail about the silk nightgown as they bent a left on 15th. There were flashing lights all down the left side of 31st Avenue when they passed. She said, "Deborah, I ain't never really looked at that girl like that, but that girl is pretty, I mean pretty. My baby got him a real pretty girl. I see why he was fighting about her."

Deborah laughed. "So where we going now, back Crosstown?"

Rose nodded. Then, slowly, that plagued image of Paul Russell hit her mind. What was he still doing hanging around out there? Had he moved back from out of Ocala? She just didn't feel right with him around. Hell, he was from OutEast anyways.

CHAPTER 17

Banging! It was like a wake-up call to Monique. Melvin! No, it was Pharaoh yelling. So she flew out the room and passed Sakena, panic gripping her when she opened up. He shoved pass her and collapsed to the floor, breathing heavy.

"Pairoh"!

Monique was scared. "Baby, what's wrong with you?"

Pharaoh barely had enough wind to get out, "Police!"

She stared out the door. "What you did?"

"They out there,"

"No."

"Close da door!"

Sakena was up this late in her Barbie nightgown looking at Mickey Mouse.

And Pharaoh was still breathing heavy when she crawled over, looking down at him.

"U otay Pairoh,"

He grinned and nodded.

"Pairoh tay he otay momma."

It was during a bath that Pharaoh told Monique what had happened. She was bathing him with a sponge. He still couldn't believe that Baser Ted had pulled over and knew if he saw him again he was going to snap.

The green Delta Eighty-eight cruised through Village Green, Forest Green, and was rolling back through.

It was the following night and Pharaoh was in the breezeway. Richie and Draco still weren't back. He looked at the green Delta then looked at the hustler approaching who was asking to hit the blunt.

"Wanted to copt some erb from Draco," said the hustler. He had on red shorts and a black bandana, "Don't know where da hell him and big Richie at."

Pharaoh passed him the blunt. He knew him but didn't know him. Just saw him out there sometimes.

The hustler hit it and started coughing. "Must've got dis from Draco?"

Pharaoh nodded.

"Dat nigga sacks fat, copt one from him da other day. Nigga showed me two big Ziploc bags full of dem bitches. And gars come wit'em now too. Say he strapped and can't run out."

Pharaoh eyed him.

"Big Richie got dat thang back there, everybody talkin' 'bout it. Say they don't know where da fuck he got dat shit from. I'm talkin' 'bout glass." The hustler demonstrated with his free hand, thumb and index finger forming a C. "Nigga showed me uh lil' cookie he bought from him, say he bought uh lil' dust off of him too."

Pharaoh folded his arms, "Oh yeah…"

The hustler hit the blunt, nodding vehemently. "In Pine Ridge to my girl house, come back to chill wit' big sis' for uh couple days, and dem niggas done got strong."

The green Delta Eighty-Eight slowly rode pass.

And Pharaoh had his eyes on the pitch black, tinted windows.

"Dat car had rode through earlier," said the hustler.

"Lookin' for dope?" Pharaoh questioned.

The hustler shrugged. "I'ont know, don't know dem nigga's either. Do you?"

"Naw…"

"See you done came up on you uh box now, huh."

Pharaoh stared at his car, and then he uneasily glanced at the hustler.

The green Delta Eighty-Eight made a right on 15th. It turned into Forest Green again seconds later.

"Nigga's gotta be lookin' for somebody," said the hustler, "Creepin' 'round here like dat."

"Ya seen what they look like?"

"Somebody said it's uh girl drivin'. Real dark skinned. Say she pretty and look fine as uh motherfucka too, and two nigga's were ridin' wit' her."

…Now when Pharaoh went back inside the lamp was on. Monique was wide awake and looking at TV as soon as he came in the room.

"Damn it Pharaoh," she cried, sitting up, "C'mon now, you always went to jail last night."

He went in the closet and got the shoebox, soon sitting at the foot of the bed, "What you doin' up?"

"Cause I can't sleep without you being next to me, answers your question, don't it?"

He picked up one of the bags that held only two small blocks of rocked up cocaine. He began studying the flakes in it. Could that green Delta be them people looking for him, Richie, and Draco? It had been a girl there. A dark skinned girl with shiny long hair. Of course, if she was fine as a motherfucka, he wouldn't know. He couldn't even remember what she'd been wearing, merely stepping over her in the ruthless moment.

Monique tossed the covers off of her and scooted beside him. "What are you thinking about?"

"Findin' somebody to cook it,"

"Well, that should be easy, shouldn't it?" She folded a leg under the other one. "Finding somebody?"

Pharaoh shook his head no. He really didn't trust anybody but Boochie. But the next time he saw that fiend in the red truck he would see about her.

A Kenwood CD player, a one thousand watt USA amp, and one Kicker 18 inch Woofer. Pharaoh was at a popular shop the next day watching them hook it up. And so he came back to Village Green bamming at six that evening, passing Peanut, who was tossing up a football. It was thirty minutes later that he got on the grind and heard the news about Richie and Draco. The two cousins had been to Deltona and had gotten rocked up. He should've known they were back. Things weren't moving as fast as they were yesterday. So rumor was the two cousins had suddenly gotten strong back there.

…Now on their way to take Sakena to see that Disney movie that had had her skipping to the advertising scenes on TV, Pharaoh seen the red truck a good ways up 15th. *Shit!* Somebody was with her. He wished he'd caught her and already knew who she'd been to. It wasn't a secret. Richie was back.

The movie was over around eight-thirty. They were back by nine-fifteen. Now if it hadn't been for Sakena wanting chocolate doughnuts, then Pharaoh would've never saw that green Delta passing Krispy Kreme. Should he go back there and tell Richie and Draco about it? Or were they actually the people they'd robbed? If not, then what had the car been doing creeping through late night?

Monique threw on the sexy purple one and ran her hand down the front of it. No sooner as she could turn around, he was up behind her rubbing her butt. Her neck swayed to the left from his kisses. She was ready anytime he wanted it.

And so they went at it for two quick minutes, then he stepped out to hustle.

Pharaoh found things slow. He went to roaming around. He saw the red truck again. This time, it was leaving and too far up when he went back there to tell them about it. He found it to be true, despite the fact that Richie told him his momma had just left. Richie had dropped sixteen and Draco had dropped eight.

As Pharaoh let it be known, Richie went to mean mugging with his gold's showing. Him and his cousin were hanging out, the half gallon of Hennessy in the doorway had them both twisted.

"Nigga's don't want no trouble," Richie said, "Ain't it cuz?"

"Fo' showl"!

"Ya think dat girl drivin' was the same one in there," Pharaoh asked seriously, "Nigga said he heard she was dark skinned. Say uh nigga told him that she looked fine as uh motherfucka too."

Draco asked how the nigga's looked. He told them that the one he had bought the cookie from had had an arm full of tattoos.

And Pharaoh knew which one that was.

Richie went to rubbing his chin. "Might be her," he said, "'Cause she had –," Cutting off his sentence, his eyes bounced towards his cousin then back to Pharaoh, "Aw... c'mon toothpick," he cried, "What I'm worried about uh bitch for? Is ya scared?" He stepped back and stretched out his fat arms. "I know ya ain't tremblin' now nigga."

Pharaoh said, "Just cautious."

"Look nigga," Richie dropped his arms, "If dat's dem people and they want trouble, you already know how we gon' bring it."

"And dat's real," said Draco.

"And uh bitch," Richie claimed, "What she 'pose to do?" The liquor was talking, "Run her ass up here to get dis dick of big Richie." He pumped his hips a little. "What'cha cautious for toothpick?" he cried, leaning with it, "It probably wasn't even them. Why ya 'noid nigga? Ain't like we touched bare faced."

Draco nodded and hollered, "Now dat there was straight to da point."

Pharaoh thought on that one a second. They did have a point, didn't they? Or like Richie would say, ain't it? That's what led him to believe that it couldn't have been those people looking for them. Who would they know who to look for? Him and Richie had had on masks? And it was plenty skinny nigga's and fat light-skinned nigga's in the city. And the car had passed him by last night. He could be spotted in the breezeway. He was pretty sure of that, unless the two cousins personally knew these people? Or Draco had revealed their whereabouts? But, when he asked them, the results came up negative with the information from Draco that he was tipped by a baser.

"Ya come up on shit like dat when ya always ridin' around tryin' to find dope for Richie," Draco said, "Both of us ain't got no license and his scary ass always think he gon' get pulled."

"You got me fucked up cuz," Richie said, "Oh, I'll get in da Regal and push dat bitch."

"You won't drive to da corner nigga," Draco told him, grilling him too, "Auntie got sick and I was twelve years old, drivin' her to Shands nigga. Where your fat ass was, in the back seat like uh bitch, scared to drive when auntie told you to?"

"Who da fuck you talkin' to cuz"? Richie went at him.

Pharaoh jumped out the way. *Oh shit!* Draco had popped up and squared off with his cousin. It had to be the Hennessy. Wasn't no way he was getting in the mix of this. Richie was mad as a motherfucka and threw the first blow. Draco weaved it. Yells of a fight came quick.

"Ya'll cousins and ya'll down there fighting," a girl hollered from upstairs.

A man yelled from down the way, "Let'em fight. They been drinking that shit and acting stupid since they got back."

The three women that came broke it up. One was very heavy set and had hips the size of a dump truck. She was the one that popped Richie on the head with a big ole wooden spoon, and she stood out there making a fuss until they calmed down.

Draco stood with his back against the wall.

And Riche stood in the grass with his arms folded.

Pharaoh watched the three boys come up. It was his cue to leave now. One asked Richie did he still have dust and Richie told him straight crack.

He better get out of there before Richie slipped and said something stupid, like Richie had almost slipped and revealed what he had taken from the girl. Now he knew that Draco had no idea that his cousin had cuffed. He told them he'll holler and left.

Rose's night had been on the breech of feelings and still was. It was 5am, and she was taking 31st Avenue up to Waldo Road in the red truck. She passed that white Datsun on the side of the road that she knew was the rock-star Ted's car – the man who'd caught a mean beating on 1st awhile back for running the police on foot. She then slowed into a right to be the third set of headlights going up that side of Waldo. Her window was down, the smell of rain was in the air, and her feelings had changed tremendously. This time, she should've woken her son up with the man's money instead of waking up the cursing Big One. She could vouch for the change of product by telling the man the source had been out. So as she continued to drive along she considered the other thoughts of why she hadn't.

Of course, going up there to get money from him was different. But wasn't it her fault that her son had strayed away from her in the first place. He hadn't been back there to check on her since he'd moved up front. No! She had pulled some strings and had made him move. She had pushed her son away from her. It was the crack, something she hated him mentioning to her, something he'd first asked her about when he was fourteen. The following years had been hell with him around and her trying to do her thing. But she knew that Boochie had been the one to tell him though.

It certainly didn't pay sometimes to fall in love with men. Lee Bernard, Pharaoh's father, a truck driver, had left her for another woman. It had hurt her to her heart, Pharaoh had only been a month old, and, what other options did she have but to carry the weight of a single mother – finding a babysitter and working two jobs, keeping the bills paid in that white house. Of course, she had raised him the best way she knew how and had only wanted the best for him. But years later, that had put a wear and tear on her, and with him going to school, that saved on the babysitter and she dropped that night shift job. She could pick him up some days and spend more time with him. However, eventually, with bills constantly rolling in, things went back the old way. It had been a break in stumbling across that job at Ester's law firm, had made her quit both. Everything had been fine then, until she'd met Paul Russell.

Rose thought and thought, heading back to that raggedy trailer in the bushes off of Hawthorne Road, her and Deborah had ran across somebody with a little money to spend.

Blueberry pancakes, sausages, eggs, and milk were the breakfast that Sakena woke him up for. Now he was fully dressed. He would ride and go see Boochie. But Monique wasn't going for that when he didn't have license and had almost went to jail the other night, so her and her daughter were getting dressed and stepping out too.

Dark clouds had hovered over Gainesville, promising the city rain, and a gray shade sat between those slow moving dark clouds. Across in Forest Green, an old woman in a tan Lincoln was picking up kids for church.

They got in and were off, Monique happy to be his chauffeurer. Pharaoh was comfortable about asking Boochie to cook it. He'd seen him cook dope a time or two.

Richie was lying in his auntie's bed when his cell-phone rung and he answered it. The house phone rung and Draco answered that. Draco was soon talking to somebody.

Richie hung up, "Who you talkin' to cuz?"

"Auntie"!

Silent, Richie didn't say nothing. What Pharaoh had told them about that girl and that green Delta was sinking in, if that had been them? The knock came and he answered it, selling the boy a pack.

Draco finally hung up. He grabbed the keys and put the blunt in his mouth, soon pushing beside his cousin.

"Where you finna go cuz it's finna rain like uh motherfucka?"

"Gotta drop auntie off some money"!

Richie shook his head and closed the door.

Rose and Deborah hopped in the red truck and pushed it on back to Crosstown. For a Sunday morning, nothing was popping but a little something for Deborah and a tiny something for Rose.

Rose finished and sent the boy along, waiting for Deborah to come out the bushes. While she waited, that long, ugly, gray LTD slowly rode pass. 'Move Somethin' at work more than likely. Probably the light skinned, pigeon-toed, flat-chested one from Crosstown who owned the car. The other one was from Sugarhill and was known for riding with her, but she was the big-boned, big breasted, scheming brown one. It was a saying in the streets concerning the two smokers, which was: "When the two together, they could steal ya radio and leave ya goddamn music playing". Rose had seen times that they'd come through with clothes, cases of beer, and cigarettes.

Deborah finally came back and they pushed it on to the store. If Checkers and Taco Bell were open, then maybe this part of University Avenue would be busier. Some UF students were walking in a group, all wearing their Florida Gators shirts.

And so Deborah put gas in the truck with her ten. Rose bought them cigarettes with her five. Then they were off to the notorious Porters Quarters, that hideous hood located on the southwest side of town. It was routine whenever things were slow Crosstown.

They were on SW 6th Street.

The sky was darkening, sprinkles of rain hit the windshield, and Rose said, "I shoulda woke my baby up last night."

"Why didn't ya."

Rose shrugged. She already knew why, but said, "'Cause I was all kinda names to the Big One."

Deborah chided, "Is he that bad?"

"Caught me early some morning's ago when you dropped me off, cursin' about that money I owed him. So I went up there and got it from my baby. He was sleep. The girl had gave it to me then girl. Probably thinking momma tryin' to spend all his lil' money up, cause that's forty dollars she done gave me."

Now Porters was dead too. Two drag queens drifted up 4th Avenue, and the homeless straggled across Main to seek out the shelter of the St. Francis House. They turned corners and everything seemed stiff. However, as they kept bending more corners, things changed. This time, it was Rose in a bootleggers house and Deborah waiting in the truck for her.

She finally came out with some Old Milwaukee, hopped in, and gave Deborah one.

"What took you so long?"

"Twenty dollars and uh hit girl, the old man had to get him some too."

And so they sat in the truck and took hits, drunk beer and rode around Porters some more. Nothing else was happening, so they tailed it to the hoodlum regions of the Spring Hill ghetto.

They were on SE 9th Street.

The wind was light, a smoker was riding a bicycle and pulling into a yard, and Rose said, "I already know what he gon' say if I come to him, momma I ain't got nothin', momma you need to stop, ya told me you was gon' quit momma. Momma, Momma, Momma,"

Deborah looked at her. "Is you alright Rose?"

Rose gestured with a hand up. "Girl... he been on my mind all morning."

…And so the rain started coming down when Deborah was taking Rose home. Twinkles of flash lightning shimmered in the sky, seeming to plague SE 15th St. with memories from the remnants of the abandoned and unforgotten Kennedy Homes. By the time they got to Village Green it was beginning to look like the monsoon.

Rose was soaked by the time she made it in. She would get herself some sleep.

By nine o'clock that night, the rain hadn't left. A tornado watch had been issued for several counties, Alachua being one of them.

Monique laid on him and kissed him. "Baby, you ain't gotta keep feeling like that."

"Dat nigga just hauled ass and ain't tell me shit."

"But baby, don't worry about it. The most important thing is I'm right here and you got me." She searched his eyes. "And I love you Pharaoh, and Sakena is crazy about you."

That night, Monique started telling him how she really felt about him, making him feel good.

…And so the tornado watch was still in effect the following morning. With a gray sky, high winds, and off and on showers, Pharaoh had ignored the flood warnings and was coming back from the Clock restaurant with breakfast.

A fresh accident in the middle of 23rd and 15th held up quite a few cars. The police hadn't arrived yet and Pharaoh d-bowed his way into the turn and kept going. But when he thought it was who he thought it was, coming up the sidewalk by Smoky Bear, he slowed down to get a good look, then, came to a stop shaking his head. *Man… she goin' crazy,* He cracked the window and yelled, "Momma, get in da car and get outta dat damn rain." When he saw her looking crazy, he hollered, "C'mon mah!"

Rose finally got in and closed the door, "Hey baby,"

"Mah, why is you walking in da rain?" He pulled off, shaking his head at her damp clothes and sandals, "It's uh tornado watch mah."

"I know," she urged, "Who car you driving"?

"This my car mah."

"Your car," she yelped, and started staring around. The music was low and vibrating through the seats. *Huh!* She started thinking. "Well, I was going up the road here. Ya busy? Turn around, I need'cha to run me Crosstown."

"Mah, dat ain't up da road."

"I know baby," she told him, thinking about asking him. But she decided not to, "So how you and Monique? Did she tell ya I came by?"

"Yeah, she told me mah." He started glancing at her, "Mah, what'cha goin' to Crosstown for?"

"I'mma stop soon baby." A guilty impression of what she was lowered her spirits. She peered out the window, embarrassed about what she'd turned into.

"Mah…"

Boy, don't start. She said, "Huh," She continued to gaze out the window, ashamed to look at him. And when they turned into the projects she just peered at the rain.

"Mah, do you know how to cook?"

Rose suddenly looked at him. "Boy, what's wrong with you? You think I done forgot how to cook as much as I use to feed your hungry ass? Not to mention I use to work at Denny's boy."

"No… momma," He giggled, "Do you know how to cook, dope?" When she burst out laughing, he gazed at her confusingly. *Man… momma trippin'.* He parked and stared at her. "What's funny mah?"

"That was uh dumb question to ask uh smoker." She leaned against the door, folding her arms with a slight grin, yet, she gazed at him mysteriously, upholding a serious look. "Boy, why are you asking momma that?" She crossed her little legs and studied him, chewing on her jaw.

"For nothin' mah, just curious," He felt ashamed for asking. But when she bent down and stared into his eyes he couldn't help but feel something.

"Pharaoh," she said, "I gave you that name. I breast fed you. I raised you." She leaned up. "I was always truthful to you, mother to son. When you asked about'cha daddy, I told'cha how he abandoned us and showed you pictures of his no good ass. When you found out I smoked, I told'cha the truth." She stared at the project buildings. "Now, I'm your mother, and uh mother always knows when something's up. It's in your appearance. It's just there. You can't hide it from your mother." She squinched her eyes, "And right now something's up, cause you got that lil' puppy dog look like ya always had when ya wanted something. Now tell me. You wanted to know for some reason. Now talk to momma."

With an unnatural feeling haunting him, Pharaoh cut the car off. "I got some powder momma. I don't know how to cook it."

Rose smiled and looked off. "How much"?

"I think like five ounces."

And her head swung back like a speeding bullet. "What?" She seen that silly look of his and popped him on the leg. "Hell – yeah I can cook it," she yelped, "Boy… why da hell you ain't been… said nothing?"

Pharaoh giggled nervously.

"Where the shit at boy"?

"I gotta go get it mah."

"Well, what'cha waiting on, Christmas, New Year's? Go get it and let's go to the house."

CHAPTER 18

Her apartment reeked with the stale odor of cigarette smoke. Empty beer cans were sitting on the scarred up brown coffee table along with two ashtrays full of butts. The faded green sofa had burn marks everywhere. The brown love seat still had the two mix-match green and yellow cushions. The old stereo remained in the corner with old phone books piled on top of it. The TV still had the clothes hanger hanging out of the broken antenna.

It had been awhile since Pharaoh had been back there to his mother's apartment, since three days after he had moved to get the rest of his belongings. Here he'd spent the last four years of his life growing up, hanging out with Boochie.

And Richie and Draco were just a section away.

"Baby, momma ain't cookin' all of this."

"Why not mah"? He walked in the kitchen.

"Cause you can cut it, and this can take uh good… cut. With the shit some of these nigga's got floating around here, baby, you'll have ya some good… powder. Cause this good dope. Real good dope. And where ya got it from?"

The shoebox was on the counter beside a dirty plate. Rose had a hunch and a partial smile. The hit she'd had to argue with him to get was the same stuff the Big One had.

Pharaoh was lost for words, stuck like he didn't know nothing.

So Rose came with, "The Big One."

"Why ya say dat mah?"

"Cause I saw ya one night leaving from back here. Momma ain't slow now." She sort of leaned towards him, saying in a sort of whisper, "So the Big One fronted you all of this?"

"I bought it from him mah."

"You bought it from him," she cried, "And where you got the money from?"

"Been hustlin' mah"!

"Uh-huh," she sung, "Been hustlin'." Rose scratched her head. Now had her son really been doing this much hustling lately? She dropped the thought, saying, "Well, you need to go buy you some baggies. And where ya scale?"

"Ain't got nam mah"!

"Well, ya need to buy ya one. We need some more baking soda too, and –." She saw his look. "Boy, let's go. Do momma gotta show ya everything."

The trip didn't take long at all. They were back in an hour.

Rose told him what to do while she operated on the stove; paying close attention to rather his phone conversation with Monique was sidetracking him. But once she realized he was listening she smiled at him and went straight to work.

When she sampled the first cookie she figured it was better than the piece he'd given her. When she saw 7.8 on the scale, she said, "Baby, we finna boom!" After the sixth cookie, she tasted some of the cocaine he'd cut. "That's good. See how ya made two, and it's still good… dust."

"Mah, you crazy"!

"Uh shit… boy, you must don't know what'cha got. Bag ya up uh eight-ball, sixteenth, some grams. Uh whole… lot of twenties. Make'em point three though, fat… twenty sacks. That uh get nigga's attention, cause baby, when momma get through, we finna ride."

The knock came when she was cutting down the stove and was about to take a hit. She opened the door and did a little dance for Deborah. It had happened just like that.

And Pharaoh was just getting off of the phone when he saw her. Now he knew what that snickering had been all about. And his momma didn't say much when he looked at her either. All he got was the eye.

…And so it was an hour later when they hit the murky streets of Crosstown in Pharaoh's car. The rain was still off and on, and, they were by Mom's Kitchen when Rose found out that he had been riding with Ted. That long, ugly, gray LTD had been a surprise to him. The passenger was the big breasted sort of cute one who'd shot out of the room butt naked.

And so the wind was strong when they left Crosstown and went to Porters a few hours later. The sky remained the same shade of gray, but the rain had died by the time they pulled up to a crack-house in the Spring Hill ghetto.

Rose went in and pulled the boys out of the house. She knew them. She introduced them to her son, and then she explained what the business was. She gave two boys, known for snorting powder, a twenty sack to bump together, watching one thump the bag while the other mentioned how fat it was. After she showed them some of the crack and told her son to get out the car, she let them know that he had quarter ounces for two-twenty-five.

Pharaoh wasn't familiar with either one of them. But after one of the boys told him the powder was naked, he began conversation with them. Before long, he was selling a sack and his mother was advertising a cookie.

"I'm tellin'ya," Rose was saying, "Ya'll bedda jump on it. My baby got that heat…" She sat it on the hood, "Two-twenty-five now, and we got fifty packs and hundreds."

The boys were calm and straight gutter. One of them said, "Dat's wah-ta."

"Uh… shit…" Rose said, bouncing her shoulders, "That ain't water."

Silence fell. Everybody seemed to be looking at each other, the wind carrying its stormy message. Until one of the boys called a smoker out and Rose gave her a piece to test. She knew her.

The fiend stood on the porch and out the wind, happy to be the tester. Soon as she hit it and held it in she went to bouncing.

"What dat is?" One of the boys asked.

Rose said, "I told'cha my baby got that heat…"

"Dat ain't wah-ta dawg. Look at her."

The fiend was rocking when she blew it out. She stood up straight, then said aloud, "Uh…ten….sion."

"Didn't I tell ya," Rose said, dancing a little and grabbing the cookie, "My baby got that heat dat ain't that bull…shit." She held it in the air. "Two-twenty-five now, come on, get'cha money right, cause ya heard… what she told'cha. It is fire. My baby got it."

…And so it was that evening when they got back, and Richie was out in the parking lot. The weather was breaking.

And Pharaoh, following his momma and Deborah inside, decided to stay back there awhile. When he left, the dented up black Buick Regal was pulling off. Draco was taking Richie somewhere, and whatever Richie was mad about seemed evident by the way he was talking to Draco.

CHAPTER 19

"Baby, I've been thinking a lot," Monique was saying that same evening.

"About him gettin' out and bussin' up in here"! You still on dat,"

"No," She smiled, "About school, I really wanna go and get my license."

They had just finished having sex and Pharaoh was getting dressed.

"Well, why don't'cha go, da Pharaoh got'cha?"

Monique finished drying off and laid in bed, jumping off into talk about it.

Pharaoh sat on the edge of the bed. Her excitement was inspiring, and when he peered at her, the way her breast was propped appeared arousing. Her belly button was beautiful and he followed her trail of hair down. Tempted to do it, he moved her leg aside and licked her ocean.

Monique froze in breath and all. Shocked, she searched his eyes with intensity, "Pharaoh!"

"I ain't neva done this befo'. You like dat?"

Startled, Monique softly said, "Yeah…" She parted her legs and drew them back, and slowly started smiling.

After seconds, Pharaoh got into it and started liking it. The erotic way she moaned and swayed her body moved him. He was fascinated by it. And then her quick gasps for air increased and he really got into it. As he kept licking, she shivered, and her liquids were a new taste that aroused him. He began sliding off his shorts while steady licking.

Shaking, Monique slid back, "Boy…" She closed her eyes, trembling, "Oh…shit." Tingling all over, she closed her legs until he opened them and climbed on top of her. She fell into his passionate kiss, her hands gliding across his bare back. She purred when he entered saying, "And baby you bedda beat this pussy too."

It was dark outside thirty minutes later.

Pharaoh left Monique the keys and started walking back to his mother's apartment, deciding to stop and get weed from Draco on the way. When he rounded the building their door was open and Draco was sitting in a chair. But after he paid him for two sacks and Draco went in, Richie stepped foot out the door.

"Damn nigga"! What da fuck you tryin' to do? I don't need'cha back here tryin' to put down, like you can stop my traffic."

Locking eyes with him, Pharaoh said, "Nigga I ain't on dat shit."

"'Cause ya lil' boney ass was 'round here petty hustlin' befo' me and cuz put'cha up on da lick, got'cha uh lil' box now and shit. You ain't paid nothin' but 'bout fifteen hundred for it nigga. I'm da one dat brought'cha in, cause I coulda got somebody else."

A wicked grin overcame him. *Yeah…nigga!* With deceit in his eyes, his demeanor became hardcore and he stated, "Ya know, ya fat ass might be right but I ain't stupid."

"What da fuck dat 'pose to mean?" Richie demanded offensively, "'Cause I ain't stupid either."

It was that moment that Draco returned with the sacks. And cigars came with them too.

And Pharaoh, grabbing them from him, looked at Draco close then cracked his eyes real hard at Richie. However, he decided to leave it alone and straight walked off, leaving Draco looking puzzled; while Richie stood by the door, eyes hawking him.

"Oh nigga, I get money!" Richie snapped, "Cuz, dis nigga done tried me, our pockets way fatter than his."

Draco didn't respond.

So Richie mean mugged his cousin. He finally stared at Pharaoh walking off and hollered, "Next week you'll see somethin' crushin' dat box! You can't stop my money nigga!"

"Ain't tryin' to," Pharaoh hollered back, and kept walking. He didn't give a damn and knew Richie hadn't even caught on.

CHAPTER 20

The gray Lexus trailed the dented up black Buick Regal to Village Green for the second night in a row.

Draco had been going and coming selling weed and hadn't noticed that he was being followed. All the stuff Richie was doing just wasn't adding up to him. Something just wasn't right. Richie was doing a little too much.

He parked and got out, the gray Lexus passing by with tinted windows.

Now Pharaoh's name had started ringing.

And it was evident by who showed up at Rose's door. The pearl white Fleetwood Cadillac outside was clean. It had turned some heads when it had showed up. The woman riding with the man had to be something like half black and half Chinese. Majority of the older generation knew him. The younger generation only heard stories about Crosstown Peety.

"Hey… Peety," Rose was saying, surprised. Deborah had opened the door for him, "What brings you around here?"

"Was jus' ridin' wit' da wind, was listenin' to da birds chirp."

"There you go with that ole talk." Rose sat a hand on her hip, a bit amused, chewing on her jaw.

Pharaoh was sitting on the arm of the faded green sofa when Peety turned to him.

"You must be Pharaoh?"

"You know my son?"

Peety chuckled, two gold teeth plainly visible. He was slender, salt and pepper headed with a miniature salt and pepper goatee. You could tell he was old school – burgundy three piece suit and Stacy Adams. A single gold necklace hung around his neck. "Might not know'im but reckon I heard of him," He cracked a grin, "Deuce dub sacks. What it be Pharaoh, deuce runnin' tre five? 'Bout how ya'll young generation talk nowadays, isn't it? Got somethin' out there that like uh dirty nose."

Pharaoh giggled before he could even say a word, then, sort of laughed a little. Wasn't everyday you hear something like this coming from somebody old school. Besides, the man was sporty with it. It was something about him.

Rose had drifted into conversation with Peety, and before long the thick smell of cigarette smoke forced Pharaoh out the door. He walked to the parking lot where he first laid eyes on the pearl white Fleetwood. A passenger was with him. From where he stood he could tell that it was a woman. Shortly afterwards, Peety came up.

"Like what ya see?"

Pharaoh nodded. He was looking at the rims. He knew that those were Cadillac 50's.

Peety grunted and looked at his Cadillac, "But back in my days Pharaoh, picture dis." He grinned and told him, "Afros, braids, neat haircuts, tight edge. Beard, mustache, sideburns, neatly trimmed, straight razor. Pimp hat, tilted a lil' to the left side. Diamond ring, gold necklace, diamond watch, three piece suit, shiny shoes, I mean sharp…" He paused, "In the original, black on black, seven eight, El dog, top back, hubcaps, clean… gangsta white walls. Diggin' the scene with a gangsta lean, now ain't dat sporty? You know he's da pusher." Peety started walking off, "Projects got ears," he told Pharaoh before he crossed the road. "Words bounce off da walls and the bricks make'em echo. Ghetto got eyes. And the eyes play tricks Pharaoh. The eyes play tricks."

Pharaoh stood there in thought. Then the pearl white Fleetwood backed out and he saw the black looking Chinese woman. He stared at it leaving, and then he went back inside, reflecting on Peety's words.

"We gon' have to do something in uh minute baby," Rose was saying on her way out of her room.

"Somethin' like what mah?"

She stopped, her hand scratching her ear. "Well, them three we bought from that boy ain't finna last us long, and it ain't that good either," she told him, "But momma might know somebody that know somebody. We gon' have to ride and find him."

"Dey say some boys got hit," Lake Road Slim was telling Raw'd- Up, "Say dey Patricia people, you ain't heard nothin' about dat?"

"Naw…"

"Dat's the word on Fifteenth. Dey was sayin' dat at the get together at T.B. Dem boys outta Lincoln Estates was talkin' about it. Say dey use to stay off of Kincaid Road awhile back or somethin'."

They were in the circle on Lake Road drinking Heineken, had just come back from the orange and blue store.

"One of dem boys supposed to be Patricia cousin, heard about uh jit in Village Green, nigga dey call fat Richie or somethin'."

"Yeah, I ain't heard nothin' like that, just seen Patricia and was like, what da fuck she doin' here."

"Hey, dat… bitch ain't nothin' nice,"

"Huh, she had Bobby going crazy. If he hadn't been messin' wit' her ass, he probably wouldn't be in fed."

The sixteenth of cocaine sat on the hood with a cut straw beside the bag. The twelve pack of Heineken was in the passenger's seat, five bottles missing.

Raw'd-Up grabbed him another Heineken. "Knowing dat bitch she lookin' for him," He raised his brows, profoundly adding, "…And ain't gon' stop until she find him."

They sat there talking and doing their thing, just hanging out like they sometimes did.

CHAPTER 21

It was Sunday, two nights later, and not a mild breeze penetrated the humid night air. Absent was just a faint touch of wind. A wicked glow was in the heart of it. Movements posed as sneakiness in the glare. Glimmery stars furnished the sky. A full moon sat directly over Sugarhill.

The box Chevy was silent except for the soft humming of the AC. Smoke danced from the Newport between her fingers. Her right hand gripped the steering wheel. The hands on the clock on the dash read 11:58. The speedometer was just below 5mph as they approached the exit, passing a parked police car.

Paranoid, Pharaoh gazed into the rearview at the police car just before they pulled out. His mother had made it happen. They had been through five dope boys to finally meet up with a big dope boy she knew. He answered his phone. Monique was worried about where he was.

The store on the corner was closed and two addicts loitered by the pay phones. Just at the red light, a wino came staggering across the street sipping on a bottle of grape MD 20-20.

Rose slowed and eased into the right turn. "Boy, you look scared."

"Not really mah."

"Uh-hu," She grinned, speeded up, and eyed him with the light of adventure, "Momma know how to do it, don't she?"

A little nervous, Pharaoh said, "Mah, man…" At that moment, the white Acura passed and all he could make out was dreads. It honked and made a left a short ways down, proceeding into the bowels of the Spring Hill ghetto. Pharaoh didn't know what to say. He hadn't planned on going all in. But when she had told him to bring everything he had, he did without asking questions. She had put her eight hundred with his, which had brought him to ten stacks and a half, to find out when they caught up with Dread that they were five hundred short for a half kilo. But things went well for the sake of his name ringing and the fact that his mother somehow knew Dread. And Dread had told them to meet him in Sugarhill, where they'd met him and handled business.

"Uh half uh brick baby. Don't panic. Shit getting good… now," *My Pharaoh*. "It ain't bedda than that other shit ya had but it's good… shit too."

"Mah, you crazy"!

"Uh… shit… Baby it's on. Momma finna do uh whole bunch of cookin' tonight and her son finna cut uh whole… lot of coke." She hit her Newport. "Baby, when you got shit like this, you ain't small time no mo'. Momma gon' keep it pumpin'. You gon' have to look out for momma and momma gon' have to look out for you. That shit you and Linda nephews going through –."

"It ain't Draco. It's Richie mah."

"Well, let it go. This shit here is serious. You already got a lot of people talking about'cha, and ya getting big if Dread heard 'bout'cha." She hit her Newport. "Now, momma ain't about getting robbed, so, soon as we get some money, we gon' have to get us some big, big, big pistols."

"Mah, you trippin'"!

"Uh shit…" She popped him on the leg. "Wake your ass up Pharaoh. This is the dope game boy, momma know. I've been smoking this shit for years and know game… you don't know." She eyed the road, observing the intersection as they crossed University. "Shit is serious when ya dealing dope boy, nigga's kill you for this shit. Gotta do like the rapper ya liked, Tupac. Hail Mary, ride or die, ride or die. Hail Mary! Ya betta ride… boy."

Pharaoh got serious at the tone of his mother's voice. By the time they turned down 31st Avenue, her words were touching him a little more.

But headlights behind them got closer and he knew that police headlights weren't shaped like that, and one was dim.

"Ain't that's Linda behind us?" she said mysteriously, "Just mentioned her name, ain't that strange?"

Pharaoh turned around. Draco was in the passenger's seat and Linda was driving – a brown skinned woman, well known for her reputation for fighting. She didn't look bad at all and went both ways. Even some men didn't stand a chance. He turned back around, "Yeah, dat's her mah."

"Uh–hu, done just got outta jail," she mentioned strangely, simply glancing around with a crazy feeling. She peered in the rearview once again, sensing it was just weird of how it happened, "Don't say shit to the Big One and get something started now, cause momma don't wanna have to shoot the shit out of her ass, cause Lord knows I will." She gazed ahead. "Had just mentioned her name," she whispered to herself. "And momma don't believe in coincidences," she told him. Then she eyed the rearview, a slight cold chill inching its way through her, "Baby, just stay away from'em. Don't say shit to'em at all."

The two men waltzed to Rose's apartment in the breeze of that Tuesday afternoon.

Deborah opened the door. "Uh… can I help you?"

The two men looked at each other.

"Who that is"? Rose asked, popping up.

The two men looked at each other again.

"Naw… must got the wrong apartment," the chubby one said.

"Well, who ya looking for"?

"Aw, don't worry about it. We'll find it."

The two men left.

And so Rose shrugged and Deborah closed the door.

CHAPTER 22

The dented up black Buick Regal came to a stop in the middle of the intersection. Draco waited for the second car to pass then made the left turn. It was 10:05pm. A sale for a half of pound up the road was getting to be a usual. He would keep bringing it, bopping to the tweeting highs of six by nines.

A short ways down the light caught him. Behind him, one set of headlights slowly came to a halt. The light had just turned green when he was yoked by the neck, feet kicking, both hands gripping the steering wheel as he fought against being snatched out the window.

Pharaoh stepped out of his apartment and stood on the balcony that night. A few people were out there, and his stare was back and forth at two of them. He hissed under his breath, anger swelling as he walked back down to Monique's. When he opened the door, Sakena greeted him.

"Pairoh back momma."

Monique came out, "Baby, are we still going out to eat tomorrow? And you know I have to do your mother's hair in the morning."

"I don't care."

"Why you looking like that?"

"One of these fuck nigga's 'round here done broke in my damn apartment."

"Are you serious?"

Pharaoh sat on the arm of the sofa. Whoever it had been had took some change. Must have thought he'd had some money and dope up there, "Probably dem nigga's out there smoking now, 'cause I know I had a bag of weed up there."

Monique sat down and listened to him. Now this here was serious.

When Draco finally came through he felt an intense pain at the top of his head, and the blurred images of two figures was confusing to him, as well as their muffled voices. He finally came through more and more, and it wasn't long before he realized that he was in a garage somewhere, tied to a chair, a green Delta Eighty-Eight to the left of him, two men talking in front of him. And then a door opened and closed.

"Get that piece of shit from around here and ya'll drop it off somewhere."

Draco had already been looking at the man with the arm full of tattoos. The other one was short and chubby. And then she whirled around and slapped him in the face.

"Gone 'head and spit it out dummy, cause people seen that raggedy ass car."

Draco was terrified. He started stuttering for a few seconds before he jumped off into telling everything.

The two men had been silent all this time. The girl had been the one doing all the talking. She was older, jet black and had the look as if a sexy, successful business woman.

Then the one with the arm full of tattoos spoke, "So you come get somethin' from me and you wanna –."

"Shut up Tattoo! I come up here to pick up and get robbed. Got uh fat motherfucka standing over me playin' in my pussy. My period shoulda been on." She had a look of disgust, her mouth open and eyes on her prey, "You know you dead right, down the way we chop up lil' motherfucka's like you."

Draco was horrified, and as he sat trembling, he was trying to talk his way out of it. But it seemed useless. Fear gripped him more and more. It seemed that it was no way that this was actually happening.

"Chubby, put a bullet in his head and put him in that damn trunk of his, and take that raggedy ass piece of shit and ya'll go drop it off somewhere."

CHAPTER 23

"Where da hell is Draco with my damn car? I told him I was supposed to go somewhere this morning."

Richie shrugged. He was beginning to get mad. Draco was supposed to take him to pick up his car at ten.

"He probably to some bitch house, and ain't no tellin' who and what ya'll done had up in here,"

Richie sat on the stool. He was looking at a magazine with guns in it.

"Get'ur fat ass up and go to cleaning. Got my house looking like this, two grown ass motherfucka's, and I'mma tell' him about his ass too when he get here. Ya'll know betta than this shit, filthy asses."

When Monique parked the box Chevy, she followed Pharaoh's gaze. "You think they did it?"

"Something tellin' me they did."

"Pharaoh, if you don't know for a fact, don't say nothing to them because you might be wrong,"

"I got dat feelin'."

Monique bit her bottom lip and looked at him. "I don't know Pharaoh. I love you and I just don't want you to get in any trouble. Plus you could be wrong."

Pharaoh looked at her. "Man… who side you on?"

Monique frowned. "I'm on your side Pharaoh. But it makes no sense to do something about it when you really don't even know. And don't ask me what side I'm on again. It's very clear."

"You mad?"

"Pharaoh," She sighed, "Just stay in the car, I'll be right back."

Monique was going to get her hair bag. Earlier, Rose had told her to come back around two. They'd just come back from eating at Olive Garden. Sakena was asleep in the back seat. She hadn't stayed awake half the ride up Archer Road.

Pharaoh was still watching the boys when Monique came back.

"Pharaoh, just leave it alone."

They went to his mother's apartment, where Monique started doing Rose's hair. It took a good while. Deborah was there, and after Rose hurried to the bathroom to look at herself, Monique offered to do Deborah's hair too.

"Girl, you good," Rose shouted from the bathroom, "Look at me." She went to bouncing her shoulders in the mirror. She then came out the bathroom doing a little dance. She looked at Deborah, then Monique, then her son. "Momma still got it don't she?"

Pharaoh laughed. His mother's hair was short and Monique had it looking like a divas. She was good. And he wondered how she would make Deborah's hair look now.

"Girl… you ain't gon' be able to tell me shit now," Rose said, bouncing her shoulders, "Deborah, we going out tonight."

Richie walked out to the parking lot. He was heated. Draco had been supposed to have been back. His auntie had caught a ride, and he just knew his cousin was hating on him; mad because he had more money than him. That was the only thing that Richie could come up with. Draco had been acting funny towards him anyway. Wasn't his fault his cousin didn't know how to sell dope. He figured Draco hated to see him getting money.

It didn't matter though. He'll catch a ride and drive his car back like he'd planned too. He wasn't scared, and when he seen his cousin, he would talk shit and laugh at him.

"What are you thinking about?"

Pharaoh sat up, "Gettin' da fuck from 'round here."

They had left his mother's about an hour ago. Rose and Deborah had taken off, and they'd both been dressed nice.

"To tell you the truth Pharaoh, I don't like being out here. I mean, I'm not use to this, not trying to down anyone, but this is definitely not a good environment."

"Before we moved out here, me and momma use to stay by Westside Park, I use to wish we could go back there all the time. Use to go to the park when I wanted too." He flipped through the channels. "Momma use to have this fish in the tank, every time you put more fish in there, he kill'em, so he ended up being the only one in the fish tank. We called him Killa."

Monique smiled and listened to him.

"I had everything I can think of. I remember momma bought me this raw ass jacket. I wore that joker till momma made me stop wearing it. The sleeves had done came up to here."

Monique laughed. He was pointing about three inches behind his wrist. "That's because you grew Pharaoh. You thought you would wear it forever."

"Showl did." He laughed. "Momma threw dat thing away. I was mad too. But then we went to JC Penny's. And this one she bought me killed dat one. When I went to school, everybody wanted one." He stopped on a channel. Wasn't really anything on TV, so he went to talking, "People thought we were rich"!

"Really"!

Pharaoh nodded. "Momma had a Benz, all black. When she took me to school and dropped me off, even the principal knew who car that was."

Monique made comments while he steady talked. Wasn't nothing really else to do.

Richie gave the girl ten dollars for the fifteen minute ride. He walked around the long white building and entered the only door sitting between two garages. To the right of him was his car – a plumb purple, '68, Cutlass Supreme on chrome assassins.

The man walked up and Richie gave him the last seven hundred he owed him. To his surprise, there was no mention about him being several hours late.

"Be careful, it's some power up under that hood."

Richie's last words before backing out was, "Ain't no power I can't handle," He revved the engine before pulling out on the straight away, leaving a distance between him and the gray car that pulled off after being parked on the side of the road. But he slowed, knowing a stop sign was ahead, and, he didn't make a complete stop before it was clear and he shot across. He was loving it – hitting the gas so it would jerk and letting off of it.

It wasn't long before he was in traffic, tuning the Pioneer into the famous Magic 101.3. He had CD's at home. All he wanted was a good song to come on so he could blast the three fifteens. And when it did he turned it up. Heads were turning more and more now. Before long, the ground was shaking. Two old white folks were in the left lane staring strangely. He mean mugged them and hit the gas on them. The next time he looked over he saw the back window down in a gray car. The windows were tinted. He thought he recognized him. It didn't hit him until he glanced over again and saw the gun. Before he could stump the gas, he jolted, head slumping from the gaping hole in it. His car jumped the curve and almost flipped, slamming into a light pole, slowing and ceasing some traffic.

The police were everywhere on Lake Road.

Raw'd-Up and Lake Road Slim were staring across the street at all the drama.

The red truck pulled up in the circle.

"What da fuck",

Rose and Deborah got out.

"What's going on?"

They were looking at them crazy, and then Raw'd-Up started grinning.

"What da hell?" Lake Road Slim tensed his body and reared his head and neck back. "Ya'll done been to uh damn beauty salon, what da fuck?"

Rose and Deborah started smiling.

Then Rose asked, "What's going on over there?"

"Girl came home and caught her nigga."

"Does it take all them?"

"Oh, she stabbed him, almost got his juggler too. Dat nigga was bleeding like uh hog."

Raw'd-Up said, "All these police around and they still over there tryin' to fight."

"For what"?

"See that big girl," said Lake Road Slim, "That's dat boy sister, them other two girls the girl cousin. It's gon' be some shit on Lake Road tonight." He looked back at them. "Where da hell ya'll going,"

"We just riding," said Deborah, "Auntie look good?"

Lake Road Slim grunted, "You look a'ight."

"I look good. I know it."

"Me and my baby got the streets pumpin'," Rose said, "…I know ya'll done heard."

"Pharaoh," said Lake Road Slim, "Yeah, we heard. Heard about a jit out there fat Richie too. You know him?"

"That's Linda nephew."

"Oh, they say he robbed some boys for a lot of shit." Rose tensed and squinched her eyes. "What you mean?"

"Patricia people"!

"Who she is"?

Raw'd-Up said, "…Somebody you don't wanna be fucked up wit'."

Rose went to prowling for information. She would get to the bottom of this.

Raw'd-Up was listening to her. Then he finally said, "Remember when I caught all them charges."

Rose nodded.

"Well, her brother was the one snitched on me."

"So that rumor true about you shootin' that boy for talking too much."

"Right in his damn mouth," he told her, "Shoulda killed him. He told on me about that too. And I bonded out on that too. Only reason I ain't go down for dat was because he got killed and couldn't testify, last time he was seen was Easter Sunday, had went through something out there wit' dem Jonesville boys."

"Well, what happened?"

A car came up and Lake Road Slim went in the house.

"Shit… Patricia had Bobby all fucked up. This was back in the days Starlight was jumping, when nigga's use to get wooped for tryin' to come to Kennedy Homes." He paused and thought back, "Around the time Slim name was ringing in all the shootouts on Lake Road,"

They were yelling across the street. The police were getting control of it though.

"They had 'bout three or four house's back then. And I swore it was gon' be some shit when I seen her cause I had just shot her brother about a week before. But she seen me and didn't even say nothing. 'Bout two days later, they found him in the bushes."

"What that mean?"

"Listen, that man got caught on Newberry Road with a whole brick, three days later he was out, few days later they kicked my door down, then picked up Lil' Elmo outta Sugarfoot. Dem boys' outta Sugarfoot was hunting him like dogs, but Patricia beat'em to it. She was spotted talking to dat jit in Kennedy Homes."

"I'm still not getting it."

"Rose, a few days after her brother got killed, that jit she was talking to had dope, money, and a brand new Grand Marquis. And don't nobody know where he got it from, nobody, that nigga was loose. Came down fifteenth flushin' that Grand Marquis, all in Duval, ridin' through Lake Road, clownin'. But check this out, wasn't even a week later that they found him stink in that same car with a bullet in his head, and it wasn't uh robbery."

"Why you say that?"

"Cause jit had G's and dope on him."

Rose went to thinking heavily. "Think she had him killed too?"

"Damn right, to cover her ass cause jit was wide open wit' whatever the fuck she paid him."

Rose was baffled, now was her son somehow involved in all of this.

Lake Road Slim came back out, staring across the street. "Dey finna be out here all night."

CHAPTER 24

Pharaoh caught a swing on his walk to his mother's apartment. It had just gotten dark. The red truck wasn't back but he would go check anyway. The Regal wasn't there either. Bad as he wanted to smoke, he wasn't going to Draco. He figured he would find something else out there instead of taking a chance with Richie's bullshit.

He walked across the median to Forest Green. Over there he found the real Gainesville green.

"You ain't know I had dis shit over here?"

"Naw"!

"I heard you was over there boomin'."

"Ain't nothin' like dat."

"Shit, I even heard them talkin' 'bout you in Glen Springs dawg. They know 'bout you way over there in Cedar Ridge and Majestic nigga."

The hustler sat on the steps, just in the dark out of view. He had short dreads. If Pharaoh hadn't of looked over, he probably would've missed him.

"I'll holler at'cha dawg."

"Yeah, come back and see me."

The walk back across the median was filled with thoughts. Maybe he needed to tell Monique that they were moving. After all, it was crossing his mind off and on along with all the stuff that had been happening lately. He went through the breezeway. He would tell her that they were getting out of there. Glancing up, there was a figure at his door knocking. He broke stride. He was just about to say something when his eyes hit the chubby one near the far bottom stairs to the left.

They were already locking eyes and –

If Pharaoh wasn't home then he was down there with that new girl was what the jit had told them, and so the one with the arm full of tattoo's was coming back down. Jit had told them exactly which door it was. Then, it was if he froze, as if spooked by the sudden movement.

The blast from the gunshot sent the few residents scurrying as fire spewed out the barrel. Chips of brick ricocheted off the other building from the single brick that had a chunk missing.

Pharaoh had just made the corner, stinging in his hand that felt like a piece of glass had just cut him. It was them.

Two more shots rang out.

A door opened as he fled out into the parking lot. The car next to his car. Her! A quick right in panic, shock, and disbelief. The distance was more than thirty yards when a shot came with burning in his lower back. He almost fell, agonizing pain as he staggered around the corner of the next section of buildings, dizziness and light headedness overpowering his strong will to keep running. But he made it to the other side. The headlights of the car that turned in off 31st appeared dim and fading. Then he soon collapsed.

The two men rounded the building and stopped at the sight of a police car. It had come to a halt. They ducked back out of plain view and started going back the way they came, casually.

Patricia stood at the opposite corner, watching. The snub nose 38 had hit its target but it wasn't enough. She seethed with rage, turning around and walking off, meeting up with Chubby and then Tattoo, who had been itching to let loose the Desert Eagle 44.

Flashbacks. The gunshots, the banging on her door by the neighbor, the panic and fear gripping her, the sight of Pharaoh laying in the road not moving, the sirens. The emotions she went through running the light to catch up with it. They wouldn't allow her to ride with Sakena in the back of the ambulance with him. She had only been back home once.

Rose sat there for the second day. It had been all on the news. And the Big One had been shot in the head while driving. Investigators were trying to get more information on that. They were already stating drug related. The police had been in asking them questions. What Monique had told them was she simply didn't know. Doctors hadn't allowed them to speak to her son yet. He was under too much medication. The bullet had barely missed his spine. They were still in intensive care. Rose was distraught. It was everywhere on her face. And she hadn't had a hit since the news came and she'd come hurling out of crosstown. She looked at Monique. That girl really loved her son, and her daughter was coloring.

The door opened.

A doctor came in and checked everything then left.

Then Deborah came in with lunch from downstairs.

By the following morning, they anticipated a similar broadcast with no new information. But body found in trunk was the first thing being aired. Chills went through Rose's body. Her eye's widened. It was Linda's car they found in some woods on 441. The Small One.

Monique got up. His head moved and now his eyes were opened

And then Rose popped up on the other side of him. She was worried and possessed that look – the old look with the addition of chewing on her jaw.